BEACON STREET GIRLS

This book belongs to:

VERITAS AMICITIA GAUDIUM
truth friendship fun!

Who's Who

BSG

Katani Summers
a.k.a. Kgirl ... Katani has a strong fashion sense and business savvy. She is stylish, loyal & cool.

Avery Madden
Avery is passionate about all sports and animal rights. She is energetic, optimistic & outspoken.

Charlotte Ramsey
A self-acknowledged "klutz" and an aspiring writer, Charlotte is all too familiar with being the new kid in town. She is intelligent, worldly & curious.

Isabel Martinez
Her ambition is to be an artist. She was the last to join the Beacon Street Girls. She is artistic, sensitive & kind.

Maeve Kaplan-Taylor
Maeve wants to be a movie star. Bubbly and upbeat, she wears her heart on her sleeve. She is entertaining, friendly & fun.

Ms. Razzberry Pink
The stylishly pink proprietor of the "Think Pink" boutique is chic, gracious & charming.

Marty
The adopted best dog friend of the Beacon Street Girls is feisty, cuddly & suave.

Happy Lucky Thingy and alter ego Mad Nasty Thingy
Marty's favorite chew toy is known to reveal its alter ego when shaken too roughly. He is most often happy.

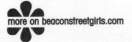

more on beaconstreetgirls.com

BEACON STREET GIRLS

Be sure to read all of our books:

BSG Special Adventure Books

First Edition

The characters and events in this book are fictitious.
Any similarity to real persons, living or dead, is coincidental and not
intended by the author. References to real people, events, establishments,
organizations, products, or locales are intended only to provide a sense
of authenticity, and are not to be construed as endorsements.

Series Editor: Roberta MacPhee
Art Direction: Pamela M. Esty
Book Design: Dina Barsky
Illustration: Pamela M. Esty
Cover photograph: Digital composition

Produced by B*tween Productions, Inc.
1666 Massachusetts Avenue, Suite 17
Lexington, MA 02420

ISBN: 1-933566-02-7

CIP data is available at the Library of Congress
10 9 8 7 6 5 4 3 2 1

Printed in Canada

൭

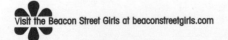

Visit the Beacon Street Girls at beaconstreetgirls.com

BEACON STREET GIRLS

fashion frenzy

CR

PART ONE
OPPORTUNITY KNOCKS

CHAPTER 1

ଓ

BREAKING NEWS

ISABEL PURSED HER LIPS and whipped around to face her friends. "OK, girls, tell me honestly. When I wear my hair like this, do I *sorta* look like Dina B?" Isabel had twisted her hair up using one of her colored pencils. Two long, black ringlets cascaded in front of her ears.

Maeve studied Isabel intently. "Yeah Isabel, you actually look a *lot* like Dina B! Now you just have to get those dance moves down!" Maeve put her hands on her head and swirled her hips around to demonstrate. "Try that." Isabel, who studied dance when she was younger, hopped right on it.

The Beacon Street Girls were jazzing up their Saturday pizza night by adding a little twist. On this occasion, they decided to celebrate their favorite "idols." Charlotte had chosen Pamela Starrett, a writer whose new fantasy books for kids were flying off the shelves at bookstores everywhere. To honor Ms. Starrett, Charlotte had brought a copy of her latest book, *Genie of the Enchanted Cave*.

Maeve had a difficult time choosing her idol. There were so many stars that she simply adored! Lately she had her eye on the hunky British rocker, hip hop dancer, and movie star Simon Blackstone. In his new action movie, *The Swashbuckler*, Simon Blackstone had been absolutely divine. But despite Simon's gorgeous brown eyes, he wasn't as much of an idol to Maeve as Rini Miller.

Rini was one of the new rising teen stars, and she did everything! She was starring in a TV show, singing in a new music video, and was even rumored to have a movie deal in the works. Maeve couldn't believe that Rini was only 14, just a little older than the BSG, and was already working so much! Maeve thought that the coolest part about Rini was that she was just a regular girl from Boise, Idaho who was discovered when she played Sandy in her school's production of *Grease*. She was living Maeve's ultimate fantasy.

Isabel had no trouble deciding on her idol *de jour*. She had selected, and was apparently attempting to dress as, Dina B, her favorite Latina singer. With her beautiful, dark hair and chestnut brown eyes, Isabel very much resembled the songstress who was topping all the pop charts.

Isabel plucked the pencil out of her 'do and let her hair tumble beneath her shoulders. "Who'd you pick, Avery?" she asked eagerly.

Avery kneaded a Nerf ball in her left hand and made a motion like she was zipping her lips. "Uh-uh!" she said as she shook her head. "It's a surprise! Believe me … you guys would never guess it in a million years!"

Charlotte slid her glasses down her nose, looking inquisitive. "I wonder who Katani will choose?"

Maeve giggled. "I'll give you one guess …"

Katani was still on a major career kick. For a seventh grader, she couldn't learn enough about business. Her latest fascination was with Oprah Winfrey. Whenever Oprah came up, Katani would always say, "She's successful, generous, and talk about stylish. Someday I want to own a business empire and be just like her!"

Avery looked impatient. "Hey! Where *is* Katani? It's 5:30 already," she complained, checking her sports watch against the clock in the Tower. She rolled up the sleeves of her comfortable Red Sox sweatshirt and bounced up and down in her bright, blue sneakers. Avery was always moving just like a good athlete should.

"Actually, it was 5:30 three minutes ago," Maeve said. She looked up from her laptop, where she'd started working on some math problems with Charlotte.

"So now it's 5:33?" Avery exclaimed. "No wonder I'm completely starving!"

Isabel, who had gone back to sketching by the window, grinned at her anxious friend. "I know it's hard, Avery, but try to be patient," she said, selecting a soft pink pencil. To the rest of the girls Isabel added, "You know she gets hungry faster than the rest of us."

Charlotte glanced up from Maeve's laptop to read the clock for herself. Behind her glasses, Charlotte's green eyes sparkled with concern. "I don't know, Iz—Katani should have been here by now. She knows it's pizza night."

Avery moaned. "And we can't eat pizza if one of us isn't here … and if we can't eat pizza than what ON EARTH is the good of pizza night??"

The other girls laughed. For someone so small, Avery's appetite was legendary among the BSG. Charlotte decided it had to be her athletic passion that burned off all those calories—no other explanation made sense!

But come to think of it, Charlotte could hear her own tummy starting to grumble. She and her dad had set the big flat pizza boxes on the dining room table downstairs at least half an hour ago. The smell of hot cheese and tomato that was drifting up the stairs all the way to the Tower room was positively torturous! The Tower was the girls' special hangout, perched atop the yellow Victorian where Charlotte and Mr. Ramsey rented the second-floor apartment. It was the BSG's favorite place to be together, and for Charlotte, the perfect place to look out at the stars.

"I only had half a sandwich for lunch," Maeve announced. "My tutoring lesson ran over, as usual."

"You think that's bad? My soccer scrimmage went into overtime!" Avery declared. "Where's the Kgirl?!"

Even Marty, their darling mascot pooch, was hungrily sniffing the air. He knew the girls would be feeding him bits of their dinner once they started ... that is, *if* they started.

Avery would not give up. "You guys, Maeve brought all those new CDs to show us the steps she learned in dance. You know, the ones from Dina B's new video? Do you realize if I don't eat soon, I'll be too weak to dance?" she whined. "Besides, *you all* were the ones who talked me into learning the dance in the first place!"

"Come on, Avery," Maeve teased. "Considering your after-school sports schedule, the thought of you with no energy is highly unlikely."

Isabel looked up from her sketchpad. "Geesh, I didn't want to say anything, but I don't know if I can wait any longer either. That pizza smells so good!" she exclaimed.

Maeve gasped. "Isabel is making me hungrier!"

"It's weird," Isabel mused. She flipped her sketchpad closed and got up to peer out the window. "Katani is on time for everything!"

Of all the girls, Katani was the most responsible. She was

always thinking about going into business or marketing—serious things that required her to be responsible. Katani liked to think of herself as a real professional. Real professionals were never late for anything.

Suddenly they all heard the chit-chatting of girls on the quiet street below. Maeve rushed toward the big window, pushed it open, and leaned out. Before she could say anything, however, the sound of a familiar voice drifted up to the Tower.

Someone was singing—way off-key. Strange. That sounds like Katani, thought Charlotte.

Maeve opened her mouth to call, but before she could, the girls heard Katani cry out cheerily, "Joline! Anna! You both look great! Totally amazing jeans, girls. What a fashion sense!"

The BSG stared at each other. "Help! Somebody pinch me right now! That can't be Katani ... can it?" Maeve asked in a low tone. Avery scrunched in next to Maeve and strained to stick her head out the window. Charlotte joined them, clicking the "Save" button on Maeve's laptop and slamming it shut. Isabel squeezed in as well.

Stunned, Avery turned to the other girls. "What's wrong with her?" she asked. "Since when is Katani all chummy-chummy with the Queens of Mean?"

"That is weird," Isabel agreed. "Katani usually tries to avoid them whenever she can."

It was an understatement to say the BSG weren't big fans of Joline and Anna, two girls in their class who liked to whisper a lot and make snide comments about everyone and everything. Now even Anna and Joline were at a loss for words and stared at Katani, bewildered. Katani, meanwhile, swept around them, admiring their outfits. "Anna, really," she gushed, "that shade of blue with your eyes ... a definite 10 on the fashion wow-meter. And those earrings are an

'A' plus plus!"

"Wow," Charlotte whispered. "Her earrings have parrots in little cages on them."

"Call me crazy," Maeve said, "But either Katani just won the lottery, or she has completely lost her mind!"

Before any of them could respond, they heard the downstairs door slam shut, which meant Katani was finally inside. "Whooo-hoo!" Avery cried. "Pizza!"

She bolted out of the Tower with the others tumbling behind her. They scrambled down the winding staircase of Charlotte's house that led down to the first floor.

"Where have you been, Katani?" Charlotte panted when they finally reached the bottom. "We were worried!"

Katani didn't say a word. She was now dancing in wide circles around the hallway with her arms fully extended and her head thrown back. "Hey, Earth to Katani!" Avery said, clapping her hands. "We're *starving* here!"

"Food can wait," Isabel laughed and shook out her black

My DIVA DREAM

Kgirl

FUTURE PRESIDENT AND CEO OF
Kgirl FASHION & ADVICE EMPIRE
(It could happen!)

hair, making her own gold hoop earrings bounce. "I want to know why you're late, Katani. What's going on?"

"Yeah … and what's with buttering up the Queens of Mean?" Avery asked suspiciously, flexing her leg muscles as she held onto the railing.

"That is unusual for the Kgirl," Maeve agreed, catching Katani's hand and pulling her to a stop.

"Well, whatever it is, it's gotta be something good," Charlotte said, studying Katani as she whirled to a halt in front of them. "Come on, Katani! The suspense is killing us!"

Katani looked at her four best friends, her dark eyes shining with excitement.

"This," she said, her voice trembling with excitement, "may just be the very best day of my life."

Isabel cocked her head. "Katani, are you going to tell us, or do we have to guess?"

Katani took a deep breath and drew herself up to her full height, towering about a foot above Avery. She couldn't contain herself anymore.

"I-I-'m g-g-oing to start my career!" she sang in a terrible, off-key voice. "I-I-'m g-g-oing to the Big Apple!"

She stopped singing and looked at all the girls for a response. They glanced at each other, bewildered. "Come on, guys, The Big Apple! Ya know … *New York*! I-am-going-to-New-York to be part of a *real, live fashion show!*"

"Oohhh!" the girls exclaimed, their blank looks disappearing. They all understood why Katani was so happy. Fashion and business were her two biggest obsessions. Combining them with a trip to New York was enough to send her over the moon. Of course she would be out of her mind with excitement!

"Phew!" Avery sighed, pretending to wipe sweat off her

brow. "For a second there I was afraid you had gotten a record deal!" After Katani's atrocious "song" the BSG couldn't help but burst into laughter.

Maeve, however, still seemed a little puzzled. "Wait just one moment, young lady. Do you mean to tell me that you are going to be a *model* in a fashion show?"

"No, silly!" Katani cried. "Even better! I'm going to help with the show behind the scenes!" She was bubbling over with the details now. "Do you guys remember my cousin Michelle who works for *Teen Beat* magazine? She's an assistant editor there now! *Teen Beat*'s having their annual spring fashion show in a few weeks and since I LOVE fashion and I want to own a business someday, Michelle thought that it would be great for me to come and help out behind the scenes to get some practical experience. It's two weeks from now, when we have that long weekend for teacher conferences. I can stay over at Michelle's apartment. It's perfect! I'll arrive in New York on Thursday and spend all day Friday helping Michelle." Katani finally stopped to exhale a deep breath. "It's just *too awesome* ..."

"Wow," said Avery. Even she was too impressed to worry about the pizza getting cold. "That is too cool!"

"*Way* cool," Maeve agreed. "So that's why you were late?"

Katani nodded giddily. "Michelle called my house when I was on my way out the door." She threw her arms in the air and spun around again. "Oh, I love my life! This is the most fabulous thing that's ever happened to me! Can you imagine? Me!? On a fashion-filled weekend in *New York*?"

"Hey I have an idea!" Charlotte exclaimed. "Let's look at the *Teen Beat* website and see what it says about the show."

Katani's eyes widened. "Wow, I didn't even think of that! Char, you are a genius!"

It seemed all the girls had forgotten about their special party and boxes of delicious pizza. They ran eagerly back up to the Tower to check Maeve's laptop.

Katani, the first one into the Tower, almost tripped over Marty. The little dog had been waiting for the girls to come back, but he hadn't expected them to return empty-handed. It seemed that he was the only one still hungry for pizza!

Marty froze for a moment, bewildered and disappointed, and then scrambled out of the way as Katani performed a few wild dance steps and collapsed into a chair just two feet from where he'd been standing. Marty stiffened, realizing how close he'd just come to disaster, and then retreated into a quiet corner behind a chair. He stretched out and watched the girls as he gnawed impatiently at his favorite toy, Happy Lucky Thingy.

Marty was used to being the center of the girls' attention, but at this moment they were completely preoccupied with Katani. Even Avery, who adored Marty, was totally absorbed in Katani's good news. All eyes were glued to the computer screen as Maeve tapped the keyboard.

"Check it out!" Avery cried. Maeve had pulled up *Teen Beat*'s website. The girls huddled over her shoulders, intently studying the information about the fashion show. "That's Leah Kim! She's gonna be at the show too!? Sweet!"

Katani stared at Avery, shocked and confused. "Leah Kim?" she asked. Katani could hardly believe her ears. She seriously doubted that Avery would ever be interested in clothes that were not plastered with team logos. The thought that Avery was actually excited about fashion was almost more incredible than Michelle's phone call!

Avery started to blush a little as she pointed to the picture of a beaming girl on the screen. "Yeah, Leah Kim," she repeated. "She's a rising star in teen fashion design! And she's ..." Avery's voice faded into a mumble. "Well, she's the person I chose as my idol today."

A wide-eyed Charlotte turned to face Avery. Maeve's jaw dropped. Katani was speechless.

"Is it my imagination," Maeve asked, "or did Avery actually choose a *fashion icon* as her favorite role model?"

"And she said 'fashion' without gagging," Isabel added. "This is too strange!"

Avery bounced impatiently. "Knock it off, guys! It's not just fashion that makes Leah Kim my personal hero. Look— she's Korean-American, just like me. And did you know she's adopted? ALSO like me. She's already huge in the fashion world and she's still young! *Obviously* I think she's great!"

The others glanced at one another. 'Korean-American' and 'adopted' were serious hot button issues for Avery. No wonder she was so interested in Leah Kim.

Isabel began, "That does sound pretty exciti—"

"There's more!" Avery interrupted, now completely wound up. "I read the blog on her website all the time! She specializes in designing sports clothes for girls our age and she finds all these awesome new fabrics in exotic places ... from all over the world! See, she's really interested in her heritage too. She's got tons of Korean-American links on her website. I have already learned so much from her. Believe me, she is just *too* awesome for words!"

"OK, OK! I'm convinced already!" Katani laughed. "Slow down and breathe, Avery!"

Charlotte giggled. "Hold on, you're telling *Avery* to take a deep breath? Flash back to ten minutes ago when you were dancing up my street!"

Isabel added, "And complimenting the Queens of Mean ... for real!"

Katani grinned sheepishly. But as her eyes passed over each of her best friends, her bright smile seemed to fade.

"Whoa there!" Avery said. "What's wrong?"

Katani shrugged and looked at the ground.

"What?" asked Maeve. "Katani, what's the matter?"

Katani turned away, her dark eyes avoiding her concerned friends. They looked at each other, confused. How could Katani, who had just a minute ago been in the midst of euphoria, suddenly be so miserable? She mumbled something under her breath, but nobody could hear her.

"*Que*?" Isabel asked. "What'd you say, Katani?"

"I said," Katani repeated, "that Michelle told me I could only bring one friend along to the show."

Avery seemed completely unfazed and began to do her Tae Kwon Do kicks across the room. "Isn't that good news?" she asked. The others glanced at each other and shook their heads. They all looked very serious.

"One friend?" Charlotte repeated. "As in *just* one friend? As in … you're going to have to choose one of us …" Her face turned pale.

There was a sudden silence in the Tower. Marty peered cautiously from behind the chair where he'd taken refuge. He snuggled closer to Happy Lucky Thingy. Even Happy Lucky Thingy, who looked either very happy on one side and very mad on the other, now appeared, like the rest of them, very serious indeed—if it were possible for a stuffed toy to be serious.

Katani had been so elated five minutes ago, and now she felt just miserable. "One friend," she said hoarsely. "Which means that even though I don't want to, I have to leave three of you behind. I am so sorry."

❧

CHAPTER 2

THE PERFECT COMPANION

THE OTHER FOUR GIRLS glanced uncomfortably at each other. Their wild spurt of excitement for Katani had now completely faded away.

There was silence in the Tower.

From downstairs Charlotte's father called, "Char, what about these pizzas? Are you girls going to eat these or are Marty and I going to have to take care of them ourselves?" Marty excitedly yipped back. He seemed to like the idea and raced down the stairs.

"I'm not hungry anymore," Isabel murmured.

"Me neither," mumbled Charlotte.

"I couldn't even look at food right now," Maeve choked, dramatically placing a hand on her head.

"Now hold on just a BSG minute," Avery said. "Let me remind you, THIS is pizza night. And WE are the BSG! And the BSG always have pizza on pizza night, am I right?" The other girls looked at each other and nodded half-heartedly.

"Well," Isabel added, "We do have something special to celebrate …" She placed a hand on Katani's shoulder and emphasized, "Katani's unbelievable, totally fantastic break into the fashion world."

Though the other girls tried to look hopeful, Katani just flopped into the nearest chair. "Sorry. I just feel so bad about only being able to take one of you. Suddenly, I don't feel a whole lot like celebrating."

"That's ridiculous, Katani!" Isabel protested. The other four girls looked up, startled. Isabel hardly ever raised her voice, which was incredible, especially considering that she hadn't had an easy year. Isabel, along with her sister and mother, had relocated to Boston so her mom could get special medical treatments for her multiple sclerosis. With Mrs. Martinez unable to take care of her daughters full time, Isabel's Aunt Lourdes was acting as head of the family, and she could be very strict. But, no matter what happened, Isabel hardly ever got ruffled.

Therefore, Isabel's firm tone with Katani now shocked the others. When Isabel saw that all eyes were on her, she continued, "This fashion show is the best thing that has ever happened to you. It is a fantastic break, no matter who goes with you. And I don't want you to be bummed out about it for another instant!"

"But—" Katani started to protest and then thought better of it. "OK, Izzy. You're right. Even if I can't take all of you, I can still take one of you. That's better than nothing, right?"

Avery spoke up, "Can I ask you something, Kgirl?"

"Shoot," said Katani.

"Who did you pick as your idol?"

"Duh. Oprah ... of course!"

The girls smiled knowingly at each other. "Well ..." Avery continued, "What would Oprah do?"

Katani pondered this for a moment before a sly smile

✿

appeared on her face. "I know!" she announced. "Charter a jet and take her whole studio audience to the fashion show?"

Avery threw a Nerf ball at Katani and made a siren noise. "Beeeep beep! Wrong answer. She'd hold her head up and make the best of the situation!"

Charlotte nodded. "Absolutely right. What if we draw straws to see who goes with you, Katani?" she proposed. "That way, it'll be fair."

Maeve hesitated. "I'm not sure, Charlotte. Let's think about this for a second here. No offense, Char, but you've never really been that into fashion. I mean, have you even read a fashion magazine in your life? And, Avery, before today, I've never even heard the word 'fashion' come out of your mouth."

"But I want to meet Leah Kim!" Avery protested.

Maeve ignored her and went on, "I know Isabel *might* like to go—"

"Might?" Isabel interjected. "I'd *die* to go! I've wanted to see the Metropolitan Museum of Art all my life! It's always been a dream ..."

Maeve was barely listening. "But, Isabel, it wouldn't even matter. Your aunt would probably say no anyway. Katani, I'm really the only real choice here. I've seen hundreds of movies about New York City. I could help you get around, and besides ... I'm going to be a *Broadway actress* someday, and actresses should spend as much time in New York City as possible. So there." Maeve folded her arms and looked pleased. "See, it's just like how you told me to solve the math problems, right Charlotte? Logic!"

"Logic?" Charlotte's eyes widened. "Maeve, how is this for logic? I want to be a *writer*. Think what I could learn at *Teen Beat* magazine ... even in just one weekend! I could do a special assignment for *The Sentinel* on the fashion show. And

P.S.—my dad and I spent plenty of time in New York when we first moved back from Paris, and I know the whole bus and subway system inside and out. It makes just as much sense for me to go with Katani!" All the BSG stared at Charlotte. It was unlike her to be so forward. Charlotte, on the other hand, was secretly pleased with herself for standing up for what she wanted. Before meeting the BSG she never would have been confident enough to say anything.

But Katani didn't say a word. Nothing she could say right now would be helpful anyway, she thought. On the other side of the room, Marty, who had made his way back upstairs, buried his little head between his paws. The girls didn't even notice him as they went on, their voices becoming louder and louder.

"Hey!" Avery protested. "It just so happens that I've been dreaming about visiting the Statue of Liberty. And Leah Kim is my *idol*; I'd give anything to meet her. Besides, New York can be dangerous! Katani needs someone who knows a few Tae Kwon Do moves!"

She gave a demonstration that almost knocked over the computer. Maeve suppressed a giggle.

Charlotte made a dive to save the wobbling desk. "Careful!" she cried.

Isabel turned to Maeve and said calmly and thoughtfully, "You know, Maeve, my Aunt Lourdes has lightened up a lot lately. My mom would totally let me go if I were with a friend in a supervised setting, like the Metropolitan Museum. And guess what? I bet Aunt Lourdes would too! Unlike all of you, I've never been to New York. It's an important place for artists to go! Especially for the show. Fashion has a lot to do with art, you know."

"Hey!" Maeve cut in. "I love fashion too, remember?

❀

Does anyone in the BSG wear more outrageous outfits than yours truly? And don't I know the most here about celebrities—who will definitely be at the fashion show?"

From that point on, everyone began to talk—or shout—at once. And as their voices become louder, Marty began barking and yipping. His little tail waged wildly as his eyes darted between the girls. Soon the girls' voices were drowned out by Marty's high-pitched yowling.

Isabel started to laugh. "Hey cut it out, you guys. We're scaring Marty!" she exclaimed.

"Ohhh ... poor little guy," Avery cooed. She scooped Marty up in her arms and snuggled him and Happy Lucky Thingy close against her. Marty lapped at her hand, though his tail continued to wag frantically.

Just then Charlotte heard her father calling from downstairs. "Char, if you don't eat now your hot pizza is going to taste like old shoes!"

Avery's stomach let out an enormous growl. "I AM starving!" she declared. "Come on, let's eat!" The other girls couldn't help but giggle.

"Where have I heard that before ...?" Maeve asked.

Charlotte agreed, "Come to think of it, I'm starving too. Coming, Dad!" she called.

"Saved by the bell," Katani said wryly to Isabel. "I thought in another minute you guys might have put on boxing gloves and gone at it!"

Avery placed Marty down on the floor with one last hug, but she was the first BSG to dart out of the Tower and scamper down the stairs. The others followed, lured by the scrumptious scent of cheese.

The girls were all thrilled to each finally have a huge slice of pizza in their hands, but tension remained in the air. As they ate, BSG concentrated on their food as though it were the most fascinating thing in the world.

Katani looked around the table as she bit into her second slice. *Everyone's upset,* she thought. *To think—I was so happy an hour ago!*

"So, Katani," Maeve said casually as she reached for her juice, "have you thought about what clothes you're going to take to the show?"

Katani started to answer, but the words would not come. The BSG were her very best friends in the world and they were supposed to be having a pizza party! Though Katani didn't want to admit it, she feared her big news was ruining the whole evening. Life was just too complicated sometimes, she sighed.

Charlotte felt terrible. She jumped up and ran around the table to comfort her friend. "Oh, Katani!" she exclaimed, "It'll be OK!"

Katani felt a lot better after Charlotte's fierce hug. "I just don't—I just don't want anyone to be mad at anyone else—or at me," she said miserably.

"We won't be!" Isabel assured. "Whichever one of us gets to go, that's just how it was meant to be. Really, Katani, we don't want to ruin your big break just because we all wish we could go with you. Forget about us. This trip is your dream."

Maeve felt guilty for making such a big stink about going. "It's not your fault," she offered. "I mean, it's great you can even take one of us."

"Maybe it would be better if none of us went," Charlotte suggested. "That way, nobody has to feel left out. Wouldn't that be fair?"

All at once, the others turned and stared at her.

"What?" asked Charlotte.

But Katani shook her head. "Look, I really want to have

a friend with me! I need one of you guys for support!"

Isabel nodded. "You're absolutely right. And at least one of us should have the experience."

"And *one of us* should have the chance to meet Leah Kim," Avery hinted.

"Avery!" Maeve laughed. "I thought we agreed to stop pressuring the Kgirl!"

"I'm just *saying*," Avery shrugged as she grabbed another slice of pizza. In a minute she was chewing away blissfully.

Katani felt a lot better. Things had gotten pretty heated up in the Tower, but now the BSG were back to normal. They all just wanted the best for her. "Maybe we should just draw straws—like Charlotte said. That way I'm not really choosing, it's just random, luck of the draw."

"That would be fair," Isabel agreed.

"I'm OK with that," Maeve chimed.

"Leah Kim …" Avery repeated, very faintly this time. Maeve blew a straw at her friend.

"Avery," Charlotte said with a twinkle in her eye. "You're going to hurt Katani's feelings."

"What?! The Kgirl knows I'm just kidding, right?" Avery argued, smiling sweetly.

Katani managed a faint grin.

"Hey, I have a question …" Isabel said curiously. "What'd your parents say when you told them you were going to New York for the weekend?"

Katani blushed. "Well, huh, they don't exactly know about it. They're out of town for their anniversary. Grandma Ruby's taking care of us this weekend."

Maeve was wide-eyed. "But what if they don't let you go?"

Katani looked horrified. "They *have* to let me go! This is the start of my career! No—the start of my LIFE!" It suddenly occurred to Katani that she had never asked for anything this big before. She would have to get their permission somehow. "I'll make them realize how important this is to me. I'll find a way," she vowed.

Meanwhile, Charlotte was lost in thought, imagining how much fun it would be to have Mrs. Fields, their school principal and Katani's grandmother, as a babysitter for the weekend. Mrs. Fields always made the students at Abigail Adams feel comfortable, even when she was disciplining them. Mrs. Fields was such a strong, positive person. In fact, she was one of the first friends Charlotte made at Abigail Adams Junior High. "She is sooo wonderful," Charlotte said aloud.

"Well, thanks," Katani said, obviously flattered.

Charlotte really laughed then. "Oops! You're really cool as well, Katani, but Mrs. Fields must be so awesome to have as a babysitter!"

Katani laughed too. "Oh, she is. And Kelley just loves spending time with her." Kelley was Katani's older sister, and she was autistic. Katani adored Kelley, though she sometimes felt more like Kelley's older sister than the other way around.

Suddenly a thought dawned on Isabel. "Hey! Are we going to dance, or what? I gotta perfect my Dina B moves!"

"Ooh! I completely forgot! Let's go ladies!" Maeve exclaimed. In a few minutes, they'd whisked the plates and cups off the table, cleaned up the dining room, and headed back upstairs to the Tower. Maeve inserted her new dance mix in the CD player and began demonstrating to the BSG the new dance steps she'd learned in her hip hop class.

The girls were soon whirling around the Tower room, scaring poor Marty, who scurried back and forth to avoid the ten almost synchronized feet. The girls laughed and joked as they tried to imitate Maeve's super-chic moves. Charlotte, as usual, was the last one to pick up the steps and the first to fall down. Katani wasn't much better. Though she was tall and slender, Katani's dance moves were uninspired. The fact that two of her older sisters, Candice and Patrice, were graceful and coordinated—one a star athlete—didn't help a bit! *Thank goodness I discovered horseback riding*, Katani thought as she struggled to follow Maeve's routine. Though the other girls laughed and shimmied in the Tower, they all were wondering the same thing. *Which one of us will get to go to New York*?

CHAPTER 3

☙

"T" IS FOR TEST ...
AND FOR TROUBLE

BEFORE THE FINAL BELL on Monday, the kids in Ms. Rodriguez' homeroom were frantically stuffing books and notebooks into their backpacks while they yammered away with their friends. It was the usual scramble with the buzz of eager excitement for afternoon freedom. Today, Betsy Fitzgerald's voice rose above everyone's. "Do you think tonight's social studies assignment will be more challenging than Friday's?" she asked no one in particular. "I get so disappointed when I finish my homework in less than fifteen minutes. It just feels like it doesn't really count."

Nobody knew what to say. It was a well-known fact among the students in Ms. Rodriguez' homeroom that no one enjoyed their homework quite like Betsy. Except one person.

"If I may," Danny Pellegrino began. Danny was the boy version of Betsy. The BSG sometimes suspected that the two could be a match made in heaven. "Lately I've been researching the French Impressionist paintings in my spare time. Monet's 'Water Lilies' has changed the way I look at the world." Danny glanced sidelong at Isabel. "I'd recommend it to anyone who truly loves art," he announced.

Isabel paid no attention, but Betsy Fitzgerald nodded vigorously. "That sounds very ambitious, Danny. I have read a lot of books about Van Gogh," she said giving Danny a smile as though they were both part of The Secret Society of Extra Homework-Lovers.

"Quiet down, class!" Ms. Rodriguez called. "Just one more thing. Please listen up for a just a minute! I have one final announcement today… an important one."

Katani had zoned out after the word "quiet." She was busy stuffing books in her backpack and planning what exactly she would say to her parents. They had come back from their anniversary weekend the night before. The problem was they were so excited about what they'd seen and done in Vermont that she hadn't even gotten a chance to bring up the subject of going to New York for Michelle's fashion show. *I have to tell them right when I get home,* she thought. *If they don't hear about it soon, they might not let me go. They'll think everything is too rushed.*

"Katani," Ms. Rodriguez' voice broke through her thoughts. "I wonder if you could repeat what I just said?"

Katani looked at her blankly. She'd been so busy thinking about getting permission from her parents that she hadn't even realized Ms. Rodriguez was saying anything important. She thought anxiously for a minute, but whatever the teacher said had gone in one ear and out the other.

Taking a deep breath, Katani courageously looked her teacher in eye. "I'm sorry, Ms. Rodriguez, I guess I wasn't paying attention."

Ms. Rodriguez was fair but now she meant business. "We're all eager to get out of here, Katani, but you really need to stay focused. The information I just gave the class is incredibly important. But luckily, it's important enough that I am going to have one of you repeat it. Can I have a volunteer, please?" She held up the paper in her hand.

Katani sighed. She took school very seriously and didn't want Ms. Rodriguez to think that she simply didn't care. This was her chance to redeem herself. Katani raised her hand. "I'll do it."

Ms. Rodriguez nodded. "Thank you very much, Katani."

Katani got up and stood tall as she walked through the aisle to the front of the room. On her way, Maeve squeezed her hand and whispered, "Poor you!" Katani didn't really mind having to read in front of the class, but it was the kind of thing Maeve would hate. Though Maeve was a budding actress and just loved being in the stage's spotlight, the thought of getting singled out in class terrified her to the core. Her learning issues made it difficult for her to read, write, and process certain types of information in the same way as her friends. Maeve's talents in other areas, however—especially dancing and singing—made her the object of admiration for many of her peers … girls and boys alike!

Katani got to the board, took the paper from Ms. Rodriguez, and began to read. "This notice is regarding the two-day school break that has been planned for later this month. Both the teacher training days and the two-day break have been postponed several weeks. Due to an error on the part of the school board, we neglected to schedule the aptitude tests that are taking place nationwide on that Thursday and Friday."

Katani suddenly felt sick to her stomach. The two-day break was the key to all her plans for the fashion show. Her parents would probably let her go to New York on a school break, but what would they say about her missing a *nationwide* aptitude test? She knew all too well what they'd say: "N—O!"

"Please continue, Katani. You haven't read the best part," Ms. Rodriguez said.

"Oh, yes ..." Feeling stricken, Katani choked out the rest. "Following the aptitude tests there will be a field trip to kick off our course on Ancient Egypt. We will be visiting the Egyptian wing of the Museum of Fine Arts in Boston on that Friday afternoon."

"How exciting is that, class?" Ms. Rodriguez asked when Katani finished. "A surprise field trip ... and you still get your mini-vacation. The only difference is it will be a tad later than we originally planned. Thank you, Katani."

Katani handed the sheet to her teacher and went back to her seat in a trance.

To the rest of the class this last piece of the announcement was good news. All ears perked up at the mention of a field trip. "No school for the whole rest of the day? Hallelujiah!" Dillon Johnson cheered. He and Nick Montoya slapped high-five.

"This is sweet!" Riley agreed. "Ms. Rodriguez, are we going to learn about Egyptian music too? I want to know if King Tut ever won *Egyptian Idol* back in the B.C.!" Riley, the music lover, cracked up at his own joke, though no one else seemed to get it.

"Please! *Everyone* knows that Egyptians weren't known for music!" said Anna McMasters loftily. The BSG looked at each other, confused. Since when was Anna the resident expert on the history of Ancient Egypt?

Anna twirled her long blonde hair and batted her blue eyes so everyone could see the dusting of glittery violet shadow on her lids. "I want to learn the great Egyptian makeup secrets! In every picture, Cleopatra looks like a rock star! I think *that* lesson would be very beneficial to *some* people in this class," she said. Charlotte thought she saw Anna glance in her direction. Charlotte just rolled her eyes. Who cared about the Queens of Mean and their makeup tips? In fact, Charlotte wondered how Anna and Joline could even see with all the gobs of mascara they wore. Besides, they looked a little like raccoons with all their black eyeliner.

Anna went on. "Egyptian queens used lots of cosmetics to enhance their looks thousands of years ago! I guess they knew the importance of always looking beautiful."

Betsy raised her hand but could hardly wait for Ms. Rodriguez to call her name. With Betsy, a hand in the air was like a free pass to speak. "You know, Anna's right! The Egyptians can teach us tons of interesting things," she said thoughtfully. "I've done *lots* of reading about Ancient Egypt and I love the museum. I even wrote an essay in fifth grade about the pyramids." She smiled, pleased with herself. "It won first prize in an all-state essay contest. Ms. R, could I make an Egyptian fact sheet for the trip?"

Before anyone in the room had a chance to comment, Ms. Rodriguez said, "If you would like to, Betsy, go right ahead. Try to include the goofiest Egyptian trivia you can find!" Ms. Rodriguez understood Betsy's drive to succeed and tried to keep it from spinning out of control.

Henry Yurt, the seventh-grade class president and resident class clown, chimed in. "Hey, what do you know? If the test in the morning is too hard, we can cry on a mummy in the afternoon!"

A groan spread throughout the class. Henry bowed to the applause from his fan club in the back row. The Yurtmeister did have his creative moments. This, however, was not one of them!

Isabel turned to Charlotte and whispered nervously, "Do we have to look at the mummies? Mummies really freak me out! I've seen waaaay too many horror movies about mummies who come back to life to hunt for more victims. When they find people they ... oh, it's too horrible!"

"What do they do?" Charlotte asked.

"They ... they ..." Isabel's voice trailed off and she grinned shyly. "Come to think of it, I'm not sure exactly. I always close my eyes at that part!"

Maeve looked thoughtful. "Hmm ... I bet we have some old mummy movies at the theater." Her father ran the Movie House in Brookline. "Maybe I could get my dad to show some for us. We could have a Mummy Movie Marathon before we go to the museum!"

Isabel trembled. "Um, you can count me out!"

"Don't worry, Isabel," said Danny Pellegrino. "Mummies can't come back to life. It's scientifically impossible! If you want I can sit next to you during the movie and explain *everything*."

Isabel flushed. Lately, Danny had been turning up everywhere she went. He was actually kinda cute, with shaggy brown hair and brown eyes. Clearly he was very intelligent, even if he did act like a know-it-all. Though the BSG thought Danny and Betsy would be a perfect couple, Danny was acting very interested in Isabel. She couldn't seem to get away from him these days. It was getting very annoying. Luckily, she and the rest of the BSG could always meet in the privacy of the Tower.

"Thanks, Danny," she said in a low voice. "But I don't think I'll be seeing *any* mummy movies before this field trip." She didn't want to be mean, but it sure would help if he'd give her some space and rattle off his facts to someone else.

Katani missed this entire exchange. She was busy wondering if her hopes of the glorious fashion show were quickly slipping away. A few minutes ago, all she was worried about was finding the right way to ask her parents' permission. And though she hated having to choose just one of her friends to go with her, she trusted that somehow, eventually, the BSG would work things out.

But now! Katani wasn't worried about taking the aptitude test. Actually, she secretly enjoyed taking standardized tests. She also knew what any aptitude test worth its salt would show: KATANI SUMMERS—businesswoman extraordinaire, fashion designer, money-making math whiz—was sure to start her own rockin' empire someday! But the timing of these tests was horrible. Could it possibly mean she couldn't go to New York after all?

The final bell rang, and the students rushed out the door. In a minute the room was almost empty. Except for Katani. She sat at her desk and stared out the window.

Ms. Rodriguez was about to lock up when she noticed the one forlorn student remaining. "Katani? Are you OK?"

Katani could hardly speak. "I can't … I have to … I mean … yeah. I'm fine."

Ms. Rodriguez looked suspicious. "Are you sure? I don't want to jump to any conclusions here, but you weren't acting like yourself today. If there's something you want to talk about … you know you can always come to me," she offered.

Katani shrugged. She opened her mouth to tell Ms. Rodriguez all about her dilemma when suddenly a frazzled Maeve Kaplan-Taylor burst through the door. "Katani!" Maeve panted. "We've been looking everywhere for you! Are you ready to go?"

Katani nodded. "Um, yeah one sec," she said, swinging

her bag over her shoulder.

"Oh, Maeve!" Ms. Rodriguez called, "I'm glad you're here. I have something for you. Would you please take this to your mother?" She handed Maeve a sealed envelope.

Maeve's face flamed. Whenever she got a note from a teacher it always meant trouble. "Thanks," she mumbled and quickly stuffed it into her backpack. She wished that for once one of those sealed envelopes would be something good!

"Oh you found the straggler!" Charlotte appeared at the door. "Come on, Katani," she said. "We're going to Montoya's." The Bakery had the most delicious pastries and delicacies around. Charlotte collected a less-than-chipper Maeve and a glum Katani and ushered them down the hall.

"I don't feel like it," Katani said woefully. This was serious. The BSG would never turn down a trip to Montoya's!

"Hey!" Charlotte said, firmly taking her by the arm. "I know you're upset about those tests! But we need to strategize. Isn't that what friends are for?"

Ten minutes later they were sitting at Montoya's, breathing in the luscious smell of fresh baked goodies. Charlotte was a little disappointed that Nick Montoya wasn't there, but she didn't say anything. After all, this was not about Nick … it was about Katani.

The girls huddled at one of the tables near the window, while Charlotte ordered them all their favorite drink—iced hot chocolate.

"OK spill it," Maeve prompted, "What did your parents say when you told them? Because if they've already said yes—"

"That's just it … they haven't … I mean, I haven't … I mean … oh no!" Katani lamented. "I've hardly even talked to them since they came back from their anniversary trip! They've been so excited that they haven't stopped talking about Vermont. I thought if I didn't interrupt them, it would help when I asked them later …"

"Good thinking, Katani," Avery said, sipping her iced hot chocolate. "Get 'em on your side *before* you ask for something, and that way they're sure to say yes. The trick is that eventually you *do* have to ask …"

"Well I was going to ask them this morning," Katani continued, "but Kelley lost Mr. Bear and got upset, so then we were all running around to find it, and—well—I never got the chance."

The girls nodded sympathetically. Katani's parents were very busy. Her father owned an electrical business, her mother was a high-powered lawyer, and her sister Kelley's autism required a lot of attention from everyone in the Summers family. Finding the right time to approach them could be a real Houdini trick!

"They'll never let me go now!" Katani added, "But hey, at least this way no one gets left out, right?" Her voice broke. She sounded as though she was going to cry for real.

The girls were worried. Katani was always so … well, confident. No matter how sticky the situation, they could always count on the Kgirl to be as cool as a cucumber. This was the unhappiest the BSG had ever seen her. Katani's hot chocolate was still completely filled to the brim; she hadn't even taken a sip! "This might just be the worst day of my life," she moaned.

"Katani, you are beginning to sound like me," said Maeve looking at her friend with concern.

"Nobody could *ever* be as dramatic as you, Maeve," Avery declared with certainty.

"Katani," Charlotte said as she reached over and gave her friend a pat on the arm, "Something could happen between now and the show. There might still be a way you can go."

Katani thumped her hands on the table and in a loud, clear voice pronounced, "I DOUBT IT."

"There has to be a way around this," Isabel insisted. "We're just not seeing it yet."

Katani shook her head. "How do I get around taking a nationwide test?"

Suddenly Maeve's blue eyes sparkled. "Why are you asking us?" she asked. "Why don't you ask Mrs. Fields? She's the principal … and she's your grandmother! She *has to* know more about this testing business than we do."

The other three turned to look at Maeve. Katani's chin flew up. "Maeve, that's brilliant! I can't believe I didn't think of that."

"You're very welcome, Katani," she said regally. No one had ever called her "brilliant" before.

Suddenly Katani's joy turned to worry. "I don't know, Maeve. Grandma Ruby doesn't believe in giving me any special favors. She's very strict about it. Just because she's my grandma, she's not going to do something for me that she wouldn't do for anyone else."

"You never know. Maybe they could make an exception," Maeve insisted. "You could at least ask her. Can't hurt, right?" Maeve was on a roll.

Katani raised an eyebrow, but there was now hope shining from her eyes. She reached over and hugged Maeve. For all her dramatic antics and giddiness, Maeve could have such great ideas. And she was so enthusiastic she swept everyone else along with her. "You know what, Maeve? You're absolutely right—it's worth a try," Katani said as she got to her feet. "Nothing ventured, nothing gained."

"I love that quote," Charlotte interjected. "I just can't remember who said it."

"Me neither," Katani shrugged her shoulders. "But whoever said it was smart."

"Hey Kgirl, where are you going?" asked Avery.

"Sorry, girls, no time to chat. I gotta catch my grandma before she leaves school for the day!" Katani had gotten her second wind. She took a swig of iced hot chocolate, threw on her bag, and in a second she was out the door.

The BSG watched Katani charge down the street back toward school. Avery saluted her and said proudly, "You gotta give her an 'A' for effort!"

ANOTHER HOPE TO GO

Mrs. Fields was halfway through the door when Katani came hurdling around the corner. Kelley had been picked up earlier by their mom for her Monday afternoon riding lesson. "Grandma Ruby! Grandma Ruby! Wait up!" Katani sputtered, jogging breathlessly over to Mrs. Fields.

"My goodness, Katani!" Mrs. Fields smiled. "Where's the clothing sale?" She knew her granddaughter's love of fashion.

Katani sighed. "Grandma Ruby, I have something really important to talk to you about." She walked her grandma out to the car and, as she did, unfolded the story of her fashion catastrophe.

"Oh, baby," Mrs. Fields exclaimed when Katani finished. "I didn't realize that was the same weekend!" She looked sympathetically at Katani. She'd seen her ecstatic granddaughter dancing around the house for the past two days after the phone call from Michelle. Now the slightest glimmer of hope that was left in Katani's big, brown eyes all rested in Mrs. Fields.

"But it *is* the same weekend. Oh please, Grandma Ruby!" Katani pleaded. "This is really important to me! Isn't there some way I could reschedule the test? You know I'm a good student. I'd take it whenever you say. But I can't miss this fashion show, Grandma Ruby, I just CAN'T! I would never get over it in a million years!"

Mrs. Fields looked down at the ground then looked up at Katani. "I'm sorry, sweetheart," she began. "I know it would have been wonderful for you to fly down to New York to help Michelle, but this is a national test, and I simply have no control over the rules. And even if I did, I can't give special treatment to family members. Katani, I love you, but there's really nothing I can do."

Katani felt as though her heart had been ripped right out of her chest. She blinked back the devastation that was about to pour out of her eyes in endless streams of tears. She tried to look strong and protested fiercely, "But, *Grandma Ruby!*"

Mrs. Fields brushed Katani's cheek kindly. "There, there, honey. I know this is disappointing. How about if I give you a ride home, we'll make some brownies and have a nice talk. Or would you rather go back and meet your friends?"

Katani shook her head. "I think … I think I just want to walk home by myself." Katani's house was close to the school and she often chose to walk if it was a nice day or she just needed time alone with her thoughts.

Mrs. Fields nodded compassionately. "I'll see you in a few minutes then."

Katani nodded sullenly. This was a major blow. Not going to New York was a disappointment that neither brownies, nor even the BSG could fix.

CHAPTER 4

༄

"FASHION, FASHION, THAT'S MY PASSION!"

KATANI'S "A" FOR EFFORT was truly earned that night at the dinner table. On her walk home, she decided to take a little inspiration from Maeve's enthusiasm. She was not going to give up so easily. Katani braced herself to stay cool and collected while she explained her dilemma to her parents. Her plan was to first tell them about the fashion show, then *after* they'd given their consent, she would mention the aptitude test. She wondered if she was being sneaky, but Katani figured that if her parents gave their permission right away, convincing them to let her skip the test might be easier.

When her dad came home with an unexpected treat—takeout from their favorite Chinese restaurant, The Golden Temple—things started to look promising. Her family was a lot more chipper than usual at the table. There was something so relaxed about eating off of paper plates and not worrying about taking food out of the oven. Everyone was soon spooning out big portions of sweet-and-sour pork, hot wonton soup, and other mouth-watering delights.

Katani's oldest sister, Candice, was home from college for

❀

a few days. At 18, Candice was smart, graceful, and athletic. To Katani, Candice seemed almost perfect. Katani secretly wished she could be more like her. "Hey, Candice, easy on the beef and broccoli!" teased Patrice, Katani's second-to-oldest sister, as Candice heaped the majority of the takeout carton onto her plate. "Leave some for the rest of us!"

"It's brain food," Candice said, winking. "I need to keep my mind well-nourished for my economics test next week."

Katani gulped when she heard the word "test."

Patrice, meanwhile, managed to get her hands on the egg foo yong first and helped herself to the lion's share. "Hey!" It was Katani's turn to protest.

"Listen, shorty," Patrice said loftily when she saw Katani's expression. "Not a word … unless you want me to fight you for the chicken lo mein."

Katani giggled in spite of herself. Patrice had a point. Chicken lo mein smothered in hot mustard sauce was Katani's absolute, all-time favorite. Even Kelley didn't try to make off with that—the whole family knew better!

While they were digging into the delicious takeout food, Katani tried to begin telling her parents about Michelle's call. "OK, Mom and Dad, you know that fashion is my one true passion—" But before she even finished her sentence, Kelley broke in.

"Fashion, fashion, that's my passion!" sang Kelley. It was pretty funny. Everyone laughed and clapped, and Kelley beamed proudly. She sang it again. And again. The trouble was, Kelley wouldn't stop singing.

After several rounds, Katani began to feel increasingly frazzled. Her parents were so focused on Kelley that they had forgotten that she wanted to talk to them. Would Kelley ever stop?

When Kelley launched into another of her favorite songs, *Supercalifragilisticexpialidocious*, Katani shouted at the top of her lungs: "I HAVE SOMETHING TO SAY!"

"Katani," her mom admonished.

Kelley's lip trembled as she stared at Katani. "You," she pointed at her sister, "are interrupting."

Don't cry, Kelley, please don't cry, Katani pleaded with her silently. *You know I love you ... you know I love you ...*

"Katani, what is the matter?" her mother asked quietly as she patted Kelley's arm.

"I know. I'm sorry, Mom. Kelley, I've just been ..." Katani reached over and gave Kelley's hand a reassuring squeeze. Kelley still looked upset but squeezed Katani's hand in return. Katani breathed a sigh of relief. She hadn't meant to explode like that, and hurting Kelley's feelings was the last thing she would ever want to do.

"I'm sorry," Katani repeated to her family. "But I have something really important that I need to talk to you guys about. I've been trying to bring it up all day."

Kelley blurted suddenly, "It's a secret. Katani's going to New York."

"Kelley!" Katani gave her an exasperated look. There was no chance of keeping a secret with Kelley around.

"What?" Her parents gasped in tandem.

"Oh boy ..." Katani took a deep breath and finally explained all about Michelle's phone call and the opportunity to go to New York. "So what do you think?" she asked hopefully when she had finished.

Her dad clapped loudly and boomed, "Well that's fantastic news, Katani! I don't see why not!"

"Hold on one second, Llewellyn," her mom cautioned. "Katani, isn't that the weekend of the aptitude tests? I just read about it in the PTA notice that came today."

"Is this true Katani?" her father frowned.

"Um ... well ... sorta ..." Katani stammered, "But wait! I have something!" Katani reached into the back pocket of her jeans and produced a neatly folded piece of paper. Katani cleared her throat and began to read out loud, "Why I NEED to go to the show and skip the test ..."

"You can't skip a standardized test to go have fun," protested Patrice.

Her mother put up her hand for Patrice to be quiet. Everyone in the Summers' house had the right to speak, particularly when they had something important to say.

Katani continued. "Reasons I must take this once-in-a-lifetime trip:

- Early start to my career as a fashion designer ...
- Learn all about the secret world of fashion ...
- Meet important people and make connections ...
- Get to bring a friend with me so they can learn
  things too ...
- Really lucky to have this opportunity ... and
- In ten years I'll never remember a silly aptitude
  test, but I will ALWAYS remember this trip."

When Katani had finished she looked up from her list, her eyes large.

There was total silence in the room. Her parents glanced at each other.

"Guess it's my night to clear the table," Candice said quickly. "Help me, Patrice?"

Normally, Patrice would have been halfway up the stairs by now. Not tonight. "Sure thing!" Patrice said gratefully.

When the girls had left the dining room, their arms full of paper plates, Katani's father cleared his throat. "Katani, believe me, I realize that this is a great opportunity for you."

"It is, Daddy!" Katani cried. "Oh, it really is!"

"*However—*" her mother took over, "There's the matter of this aptitude test."

Katani's heart sank. "Can't I just skip it?" she begged. "What if I was sick that day? I'd have to stay home from school anyway, right?"

"No, Katani, you can't do that," her mother said. "I'm sure that every single seventh grader in America would rather do anything other than take a standardized test."

"But this is major for me!" Katani argued. "Come on, Mom! I have to do this. I mean, what if … what if Michelle gets a different job. What if she decides to be a dentist or something? I might never get another chance like this—ever!"

"I don't like dentists, not one bit." Kelley shook her head.

"Katani, you are being a tad dramatic here," her mother said as she tried to suppress a smile. Katani could feel her temper rising.

Her father spoke up quietly. "Katani, I know you want to start thinking about a career in fashion, but for the time being you're only a middle school student. That's your job right now."

Katani felt completely defeated. How could they not understand how much this meant to her? "I can't *believe* this!" she cried. "I wish I wasn't a student. I wish I could just go to New York RIGHT NOW!"

Kelley, who had been listening quietly, perked up. "If Katani is going to New York—I am going with her," Kelley pronounced. "I am going to pack my bag."

"No, no, sweetie," her mother said.

"Katani's leaving me!" Kelley wailed and suddenly she burst into tears and threw up her hands. "No, no, Katani, please don't leave me!"

She looked so tragic that everyone had to keep from laughing out loud—even Katani.

Her mom reached over to stroke Kelley's hair and turned to Katani. "I'm sorry, honey, but our answer is no. You have to take the test, and that's final."

Katani's whole life was crashing into pieces around her, and her parents didn't understand a thing. "Fine!" she replied. Katani shoved her chair back into the table and bent down to give Kelley a hug. Kelley jumped up and threw herself into her sister's arms.

"C'mon, let's blow this popsicle stand!" said Kelley. She grabbed her sister's hand and led her out of the room. *At least Kelley is loyal*, Katani thought as she raised her head and marched out of the room with Kelley in tow.

EVERY CLOUD HAS A SILVER LINING

It had been a strained evening at the Kaplan-Taylor household. Maeve's brainy little brother Sam, who adored all things military and never got less than an "A" on anything, had chattered away all night about a diorama he was making on the Battle of Gettysburg.

"That sounds awesome Sam," Maeve's mother said as she worriedly corrected Maeve's math homework. "Maeve, at least half of these answers are wrong. Are you sure you were really trying?" Maeve gave her mom a pained look. "Sorry, sweetie. I am just wondering if maybe it would be a wise idea to extend your tutoring hours again, you know, just in case …"

Maeve tried to please her mother by taking on as much tutoring as possible to improve her math—her most detested subject. But she didn't want to give up the after-school activities that she truly loved, like singing and hip hop. More tutoring was pretty much the worst thing she could possibly imagine.

"You know, Mom, it really doesn't make sense," she explained, "to spend all of my time on things I am terrible at. I mean—I will never grow up to teach math or anything. And I *could* teach dancing or be in the movies or on Broadway. Can't you just see it now, Mom—Maeve Kaplan-Taylor in *An Evening with Maeve*," she said as she swished her hand across her face and imagined her name in lights. Maeve could see it even if her mother couldn't. After all, it was her destiny.

"I get it, sweetheart," her mom said dryly. "But you still have to pay your bills and file your taxes."

Maeve threw back her hair. "I'll have people for that."

"Maeve," her mother said firmly, "Focus, please."

Maeve's father usually agreed with Maeve that more tutoring was unnecessary. It made the issue a little less stressful. But her parents had recently separated, and now Mr. Taylor wasn't around to offer his opinion during any of these conversations. Maeve tried to keep her head up and not complain about anything because she knew her mother was having a tough time too. She was adjusting to a new full-time job and a new life without her dad. Maeve wished they could all be a family again … she wished her dad was here right now.

"Huh?" Maeve asked suddenly, as if waking up from a daydream. Her mother was calling her name impatiently.

"Maeve! Where is the note that Ms. Rodriguez gave you to give to me? She's on the phone right now asking about it."

"Note?" Maeve tried to concentrate.

Ms. Kaplan rolled her eyes and said into the phone, "Ms. Rodriguez, can I call you back in a few minutes? Wonderful. Thank you."

✿

She hung up and marched over to Maeve. "Well?"

"Oh …" Maeve said. "Yes, she did. I'm sorry—I completely forgot. I shoved it into my backpack and not my notebook, so I didn't see it when I took out my homework."

"Really Maeve!" Her mother sounded exasperated. "How am I supposed to help you if I don't even get the notes your teacher sends home? You're in seventh grade now, Maeve."

Maeve got up slowly and went to her backpack to retrieve the note. She really had intended to give it to her mother, but it had completely slipped her mind. Maeve hoped that when she grew up she could have her own assistant to help her keep track of all the important details. In the meantime, she figured that she'd devise a better system than the one she had now or else she would not make it through high school.

Maeve picked through the mounds of paper in her backpack until she found the envelope from Ms. R. It was pretty grimy looking, so she wiped off some of the crumbs before she handed it over. It was now completely wrinkled, but at least she hadn't lost it. For a minute Maeve felt a little bit proud of herself. A couple of months ago, that note might have been long gone. Maybe she was getting better at remembering after all.

Then she saw her mother's expression. She was looking at the crinkly, sticky envelope. "Maeve, what am I going to do with you?"

"Hey, Mom, it's not like it's the Declaration or Independence or anything. It's just a note and you can still read it," Sam piped up, not even lifting his head from his book on General Stonewall Jackson.

Maeve slipped him her last piece of gum from her pocket. *Sometimes Sam could be so sweet,* she thought.

Her mother gingerly opened the envelope and read over

the note in her hand. "This says you won't be taking the nationwide aptitude test with everyone else in your class. They are doing an untimed test on the following Monday for kids who have learning issues or who need extra time." She smiled up at Maeve. "This is great, sweetheart. You will have time to think and do your best. I'd better go call your teacher back."

But Maeve's heart sank as that old feeling came flooding back. The learning-challenged kids. The "different" ones. How long would she have to be reminded of this? Worst of all, she wished her mother wouldn't bring up her learning issues in front of Sam, who got perfect grades and never turned anything in late. School was always so easy for him, and he was so much *younger*. It just wasn't fair.

I hate this, she thought. Why can't I just be one of the ordinary, regular kids? They get to take the test on Thursday and Friday, and now I'm stuck by myself taking the test on—

And then suddenly Maeve had a beyond brilliant idea. She felt fantastic, ecstatic, like a million dollars. This was it! This could be the answer to Katani's problem!

She waited until her mother was off the phone and then said excitedly, "Mom! I just realized! If a whole bunch of us are taking the test on Monday, instead of Friday, maybe Katani could too!" She quickly told her mother all about Katani's invitation to the *Teen Beat* magazine fashion show and her crushing disappointment that she couldn't go because of the aptitude tests.

Her mother looked thoughtfully at her when she'd finished speaking. "You know, Maeve," she said, "Katani's awfully lucky to have a smart girl like you to help her out."

Maeve looked up at her, surprised, and pushed back her beautiful red hair. "She's my friend, Mom," she said.

"I know." Her mom brushed a kiss over her forehead.

"I'm awfully proud of you."

"Maeve?" Sam asked a little shyly. "If you are on Broadway, I am going to be proud-EST of you, because you're my sister!"

"Well, thanks Sam," said Maeve. She had no idea, of course, that while she basked in her mom's unexpected and sweet praise and Sam's admiration, Katani was buried facedown on her pillow, crying the unhappiest tears of her life.

❧

CHAPTER 5

S.O.S. MAEVE!

"PLEASE, MRS. FIELDS," Maeve begged the school principal the next morning. She had rushed through breakfast, dashed out of her house before Sam, and gotten to school earlier than she ever had in her life. She was so consumed with the idea of helping Katani that she couldn't think of anything else. In funky pink sandals, her feet felt like they had wings.

Mrs. Fields listened patiently to Maeve's explanation. "Since other kids were already scheduled to take the aptitude tests on Monday, why can't Katani?" Maeve argued. "See, they wouldn't be making any special exceptions for her, and all the proctors and testing rooms have already been arranged. This weekend means so much to Katani. I know it would just kill her to miss it. Besides, if there are twenty or thirty kids already being tested, what's the harm in just one more? I mean, why should Katani be punished just because she doesn't have dyslexia?" Maeve concluded, smiling sweetly.

Mrs. Fields couldn't help but laugh. "All right, Maeve," she smiled. "Perhaps this is Katani's loophole. I hadn't thought about the special arrangements we make for other students."

She was silent for a moment. For the first time Maeve could remember, she didn't flinch at the phrase "other students."

"Hmm ..." Mrs. Fields tapped her foot, "Two other parents have also requested a change in testing days because of serious scheduling conflicts. We might be able to test all those students at the same time as the students taking the untimed test." She nodded. "Tell you what. I'll talk to the test proctors this morning. They do have the final say, but if the answer is yes, I think we might be able to work it out."

Maeve's face was luminous. "Oh, Mrs. Fields! That's wonderful!" she breathed.

"But—" Mrs. Fields said sternly, holding up a finger, "I don't want Katani to hear one word about this until I'm certain. I wouldn't want to get her hopes up if it doesn't work out. Promise me you won't say anything to her?"

"I promise!" Maeve exclaimed. "Oh, thank you, Mrs. Fields!" She was so happy she wished there was a lamppost in the office, so she could swing around it and dance like Gene Kelly in *Singin' in the Rain*.

Maeve dashed out of the office with ten minutes to spare before the first bell rang. She scanned the students milling about the steps of Abigail Adams Junior High. Katani was no where in sight. *Phew!* she thought. She didn't think she could bear to have this secret inside her, lighting her up like Times Square on New Year's Eve.

Luckily, she spotted Isabel coming up the steps toward her. "Oh, Iz!" Maeve cried. "The most wonderful thing has happened!" She quickly told Isabel about her idea and what Mrs. Fields had said.

"Oh my gosh, that's wonderful!" Isabel gasped. "You have the best ideas."

"But no matter what, you can't tell Katani yet," cautioned

Maeve in a quiet voice.

"Oh, I know. But we can tell the rest of the BSG. Look, there's Charlotte!"

Charlotte jogged over with her braided pigtails bouncing against her shoulders. She was wearing one of her favorite Paris T-shirts, the one with "Vive La France" written in sparkles in front of a picture of the Seine River. "What's going on?" Charlotte asked after one look at Maeve's happy face.

Isabel and Maeve stumbled over each other to tell the story. Charlotte gave Maeve a huge hug. "Oh, Maeve, what a smart idea!"

"Smart?" Maeve said weakly.

"Yes." Charlotte shook her a little. "You figured out how to turn a difficult situation into an amazing opportunity for a friend! That's *smart*, Maeve."

Maeve didn't think she could deal with more praise, but she got more when Avery bounced up and learned Maeve's idea. "Leah Kim, Leah Kim," Avery began to sing, right on the school steps. "And all because of Maeve!" The others laughed.

"Don't count your chickens before they hatch, Avery," Charlotte warned.

"Let her!" Isabel laughed. "I think Maeve really figured out the solution, and it's going to work! Now whether or not Avery gets to meet Leah Kim, well, that's another story." The girls laughed as the bell rang, and students began to stream into the double doors. Avery, Maeve, Isabel, and Charlotte looked around. This was the second time in just four days that Katani was late. It wasn't like her!

"There she is," Charlotte whispered, nodding at the walk. Katani came up the steps slowly. Her face was expressionless.

"Hi everybody. Guess we'd better get to class." And without waiting for them, Katani went inside.

Katani went through the morning like a robot, hearing only half of what her teachers said. She dutifully got out her notebook when the rest of the class did and checked her homework when asked, but she was just going through the motions. In the back of her mind was a little voice that drowned out everything else. It kept repeating, "You're not going. You're not going. You're not going."

Katani told herself to put her chin up and stop moping. *I mean, New York will always be there*. But she couldn't seem to follow her own advice. *Get with it Katani!* she said to herself. *Self pity isn't going to get you anywhere!*

She knew her friends were giving her encouraging nods in every class, but she couldn't bring herself to meet their eyes. She hated that everyone was feeling sorry for her; she already felt sorry enough for herself. And the other girls were being so understanding it made her want to cry even more. She wished she had a horseback riding lesson this afternoon. That always cleared her mind.

When the bell rang for lunch, Ms. Rodriguez called her over. "Katani, can I talk to you for a minute?" she asked.

What now? Katani thought miserably. She feared that Ms. Rodriguez had noticed her negative attitude and was going to speak to her about it. Not that she didn't deserve it, Katani admitted to herself, but right now she didn't know if she could handle any more disappointment ... especially in herself.

Katani shuffled listlessly to the teacher's desk as the bell rang and the other students emptied out of the room. "I have some news for you, Katani," said Ms. Rodriguez.

She paused as Katani's big, brown eyes looked up at her. Katani said nothing. "There's been a change of plans," Ms. Rodriguez went on. "Katani, on Monday you may take the aptitude test with the students who are taking it untimed. You will still have to abide by the same timing rules as you would have if you had taken it on the scheduled dates. The good news is that you can have the long weekend off, as you originally planned."

For a minute, Katani didn't think she'd heard right. "Oh!" she sputtered. "I … I … thank you, Ms. Rodriguez!"

"Don't thank me," Ms. Rodriguez winked. "It was Maeve's idea. She ran it by Mrs. Fields this morning, and it's already been approved."

Katani gaped. Maeve had gone to Grandma Ruby? And Grandma Ruby had gone to bat for her and changed her testing schedule? It was too good to be true! She couldn't think of the words to express the joy that was suddenly flooding into every cell of her body. She felt like a tremendous boulder had rolled off her back. The sun seemed to be shining right in the classroom. She, Katani Summers, felt like dancing… and that was something!

Her teacher was smiling. "This must be a pretty important weekend."

"You have no idea!" Katani breathed. She quickly told Ms. Rodriguez all about Michelle, *Teen Beat* magazine, and the fashion show.

Ms. Rodriguez nodded approvingly. "That'll be a wonderful experience for you," she said. "I think it's great that you're already thinking about your dreams. I have a feeling that you're going to be very successful one day, Katani."

Katani's smile spread from ear to ear. Her eyes shined joyously. Then just like that her smile faded.

"Hey there? Why the long face?" asked Ms. Rodriguez. "You should be celebrating."

"I know," Katani sighed as she thought of her four loving

❀

friends. "But now I've got a big decision to make."

The teacher glanced at the clock. "Well, I'm available to talk about it. But it has to be pretty soon, or you won't have time for lunch. It's up to you Katani."

Katani nodded. Suddenly all she wanted to do was tell her friends all about the miracle that had just fallen in her lap ... and thank Maeve, of course!

"Thanks, Ms. R. I think I gotta go to lunch!" Katani gathered her things and scuttled out of the classroom.

The other girls were eating at their usual table. When they saw Katani come in, a huge grin erupted on Isabel's face. "I knew it!" she cried. "It worked, didn't it, Katani?"

"It sure did," Katani confirmed. She squeezed each girl so hard she left marks on their skin. "I am going to New York! Thanks to you, Maeve," she added, giving the red-haired girl an extra squeeze. "It's really going to happen!"

The girls were so happy they crowded around Katani for a group hug, which left even more marks on everyone's skin, but nobody cared. "This," Isabel declared, "calls for a BSG cheer. Hip, hip ..."

"HOORAY!"

"Hip, hip ..."

"HOORAY!"

"Hip, hip ..."

"HOORAY!!!"

"I just can't believe that it all worked out," Maeve said, the happiness visible on her face. She looked like she wanted to jump up and down. Avery was already jumping up and down as she shouted, "Go Katani, it's your birthday, we're gonna party like it's your birthday!" with each jump.

Katani laughed. "This is better than my birthday. You guys, what do I wear in New York? What kind of clothes will they be showing at the show? What will I really be doing to help Michelle? How much time will I have for sightseeing? And—oh …" The smile faded from her face as she looked at her four best friends.

"… and who gets to go with you?" Isabel finished.

Avery pushed away her salad, which didn't have more than a couple of bites left on the plate.

Maeve opened her fringed pink purse and began searching for a pen, just for something to do. She really wanted to go on this trip.

"Look," Charlotte said, "we know you'd like to take all of us, Katani. So don't get upset at yourself or feel sad about this just because you can't. And yes, we all have our own reasons for why we'd like to go, and they're all good ones."

"The Metropolitan Museum," Isabel said dreamily.

"Broadway," Maeve breathed. "Celebrities …"

"Journalistic experience," admitted Charlotte.

"Ellis Island and Leah Kim," Avery said hopefully.

Charlotte looked at all of her friends and added, "Plus we'd all love to go to New York City with you." The BSG nodded. She continued, "But the truth is, Katani, there's really only one fair choice, and we all know who."

Katani looked confused. "There is? We do?"

"I mean one person made this possible for *you*, and she's the one who deserves to go. Of course the rest of us want to, but it wouldn't be right. You should take the one who saved the day. She's the real heroine here."

No one said anything, but one by one, they turned to look at Maeve. Maeve's face grew bright red, and she dug down even further in her fringed handbag to avoid everyone's eyes.

"Charlotte is right," Isabel said, "Maeve does deserve it."

Even a very disappointed Avery nodded, "She gets my vote. Plus, she doesn't have to worry about getting out of the test. She's taking it on Monday anyway."

Charlotte nodded too. "It's just the right choice. Period. The end."

Katani hugged Maeve, who couldn't believe her luck and was still fake-looking for a pen. "Welcome aboard, girlfriend."

"Woo-hoo!" Avery whistled. "Maeve and Katani hit the Big Apple—a recipe for adventure!"

Maeve finally ceased the pen search, looked up, and met Katani's wild grin. "You really want me to come?"

Katani felt overjoyed, happier than she had felt since she got that fateful call. "Want you to come? I can't wait! It's going to be so awesome, Maeve. Just think—five more minutes of lunch, and less than two weeks 'til we take off for New York!"

Maeve slapped the girls high-five and gleefully cried, "Yee-haw! Broadway, here I come!"

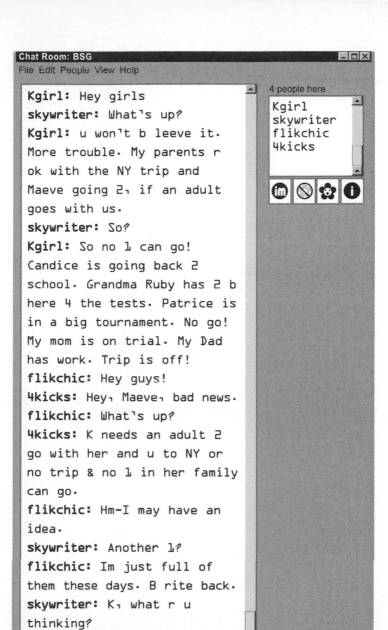

Chat Room: BSG

File Edit People View Help

Kgirl: Hey girls
skywriter: What's up?
Kgirl: u won't b leeve it.
More trouble. My parents r
ok with the NY trip and
Maeve going 2, if an adult
goes with us.
skywriter: So?
Kgirl: So no 1 can go!
Candice is going back 2
school. Grandma Ruby has 2 b
here 4 the tests. Patrice is
in a big tournament. No go!
My mom is on trial. My Dad
has work. Trip is off!
flikchic: Hey guys!
4kicks: Hey, Maeve, bad news.
flikchic: What's up?
4kicks: K needs an adult 2
go with her and u to NY or
no trip & no 1 in her family
can go.
flikchic: Hm-I may have an
idea.
skywriter: Another 1?
flikchic: Im just full of
them these days. B rite back.
skywriter: K, what r u
thinking?

4 people here

Kgirl
skywriter
flikchic
4kicks

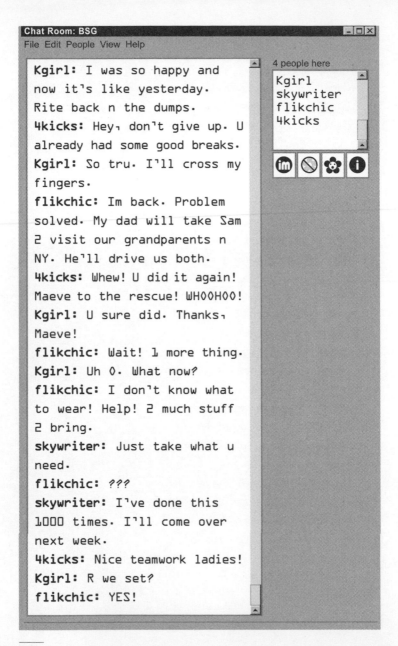

Chat Room: BSG

File Edit People View Help

4 people here

Kgirl
skywriter
flikchic
4kicks

Kgirl: I was so happy and now it's like yesterday. Rite back n the dumps.

4kicks: Hey, don't give up. U already had some good breaks.

Kgirl: So tru. I'll cross my fingers.

flikchic: Im back. Problem solved. My dad will take Sam 2 visit our grandparents n NY. He'll drive us both.

4kicks: Whew! U did it again! Maeve to the rescue! WHOOHOO!

Kgirl: U sure did. Thanks, Maeve!

flikchic: Wait! 1 more thing.

Kgirl: Uh 0. What now?

flikchic: I don't know what to wear! Help! 2 much stuff 2 bring.

skywriter: Just take what u need.

flikchic: ???

skywriter: I've done this 1000 times. I'll come over next week.

4kicks: Nice teamwork ladies!

Kgirl: R we set?

flikchic: YES!

Maeve's Notes to Self:

Sooo glad Katani can go to NY after all—
and wow, she picked me to go with her!
Does "totally thrilled" cover it? I'm
going to visit my favorite city where Meg
Ryan and Tom Hanks fell in love in
Sleepless in Seattle and where *West Side
Story* happened. Too magical!
Remember to bring back totally cool gifts
for BSG who are staying here, esp. Char,
because she insisted Katani pick me.
Char, you're way cool!
Something from Metropolitan Museum for
Isabel?
NY shirts to add to Charlotte's
international T-shirt collection (she has
a lot from Paris, so ...) Or a journal
with a NY landmark on it?
For Avery—tuff one. Anything by Leah Kim?
Or sports? Who knows!

CHAPTER 6

℞

THE BARE ESSENTIALS

"MAEVE, I HAVE THREE WORDS FOR YOU—OUT OF CONTROL!" Charlotte exclaimed.

It was the Wednesday night before Katani and Maeve were scheduled to hit the road for New York City. Maeve figured her dad's car could hold at least a dozen suitcases.

Charlotte was standing in the middle of Maeve's bedroom, but it was hard to tell where the floor ended and the furniture began, because there were clothes flung everywhere—atop the dresser, on the floor, draped all over the furniture. Five pairs of pink shoes, from sandals to boots, were tossed on the bed. A bright pink quilted jacket lay on the pillow. Boxes full of earrings and hair accessories were heaped on the floor. Maeve was sifting through a pile of blue, pink, and purple shirts at the bottom of her closet.

Charlotte was absolutely overwhelmed by the chaos. "You're going for a weekend, not a month!" she reminded her friend.

Maeve looked up. "Obviously!" she said. "Why do you think I'm only taking coordinating outfits? See? It might look like a lot, but it's really just staples, Char. Bare ... ugh ... minimum!" She heaved, slapping down a dozen colorful shirts on her bed.

"Bare minimum! Maeve, you couldn't wear all this stuff if you changed your outfit eight times a day!" Charlotte cried shaking her head. "You're taking enough clothes to run the fashion show yourself!"

Charlotte had come over, at Maeve's desperate request, to help her pack for the trip. Since Charlotte had lived all over the world, she knew all about packing efficiently. But right now Charlotte didn't even know where to begin. Maeve seemed to think that she was taking the Queen Elizabeth 2 luxury cruise to Europe instead of making a weekend trip to the Big Apple.

Maeve had three large suitcases lying carelessly on the floor. One was already full, the second more than half full, and the third contained only cosmetics, jewelry, three large hats and half a dozen bottles of shampoo and conditioner. All of them were full-size, not travel size, and would take up tons of room in the suitcase.

Charlotte took several deep breaths and sat down on the only edge of the bed that wasn't completely covered with clothes. Packing Maeve for a weekend trip to New York was a bigger challenge than packing for the safari she and her dad took in Africa! Where do I even begin? Charlotte asked herself. Perhaps she could help by getting Maeve to think logically about what she needed.

"Look, what are the things that you absolutely *have* to take?" Charlotte asked. "You know, just put together the necessities. Let's make a list."

Maeve bounced up from the floor, nodding happily. "Yeah, I did that. They're all in those suitcases, see?" Maeve pointed to the mounting piles. "I have my daytime outfits there, nighttime outfits there, and in this bag I did formal and semi-formal." Suddenly Maeve gasped. "Oh no! I completely forgot about casual! I figured I'd only take my best, since New York is full of ritzy restaurants and stuff, but what if the fashion show is supposed to be comfy-casual ... or wait ... what if it's bohemian-chic? I wouldn't want to embarrass Katani!"

Charlotte gazed at a very flustered Maeve. She had such a good heart. But oh, she got so carried away sometimes! "OK," she said carefully. "Where are your formal outfits?"

Maeve nodded toward the first suitcase. "Three long dresses, two short dresses, and one skirt, in case it's OK to wear skirts."

Charlotte coughed. "OK Maeve, this isn't going to be easy. Now I want you to choose one. Just one. You might not even need that," she added. "This is a working weekend for Michelle, remember. And I seriously doubt that you are going to eat at fancy restaurants. I mean, my guess is some hamburger places or Thai food."

Maeve looked crushed. "But what if ...?"

"ONE," Charlotte repeated firmly. "Which do you like the best?"

Maeve took almost three minutes to decide. "The blue dress. I think."

"Great." Charlotte picked up the dress. "Now you can put *aaaaaall* that other stuff back," she instructed.

"But Char—"

"Put it back, I say!" Charlotte ordered, desperately trying not to laugh.

Maeve reluctantly removed the extra skirts and dresses.

"That's great, Maeve. Now where's your warm jacket?"

Maeve frowned. "Huh. I didn't think about that," she admitted. "You really think I need one?"

Charlotte nodded. "Definitely. New York is pretty much the same as Brookline, and you know how cool it gets at night."

"OK, OK." Maeve went downstairs and came back with her favorite parka.

"How about walking shoes?" Charlotte asked, looking at the mountain of shoes on the bed.

Maeve wrinkled her nose and pointed at her closet. "Walking shoes? Ew. Very un-cool."

"Very important," Charlotte said as she picked up a pair of comfortable-looking pink sneakers and handed them to Maeve. "You know everyone in New York walks everywhere. Besides, you'll be standing on your feet at the show. Trust me, you'll thank me later."

"You sound like my mom!" Maeve wailed as she flung herself on the bed.

"Awesome," Charlotte said. "After a whole day of helping models with their clothes and hanging up stuff and running errands, you'll want to kiss these shoes." She tossed them in Maeve's suitcase.

"Please Charlotte! I would never kiss shoes that have touched pavement. Gross."

Charlotte rolled her eyes and looked nervously at the three suitcases. "OK," she sighed. "It's time to be ruthless."

They reached several compromises. Charlotte agreed to let Maeve take a pair of rhinestone-studded shoes to match the blue dress ICOF (Maeve's acronym for "in case of formal"). In return, Maeve agreed to leave the majority of her pink shoe collection at home. Instead of the dramatic floor-length nightgown, Maeve packed an oversized T-shirt for pjs. Charlotte, in exchange, allowed Maeve to take one hat (it was better than nothing) and a pair of long, silk gloves. Maeve packed several sets of underwear and socks and reduced the toiletries to a toothbrush and toothpaste, dental floss, shampoo, conditioner, and soap. Charlotte approved the final load, except for one thing: "What did I tell you about the big curlers, missy of the already curly hair? They stay!"

Maeve insisted that she couldn't cut down on her clothes unless she brought more accessories to "dress them up." She sorted out earrings, rings, bracelets, scarves, and two handbags, and also packed six pairs of pants, two pairs of jeans, eight shirts, and three sweatshirts. The results were now sloppily stuffed into two of the wheeled suitcases. Charlotte knew she'd open them up again to wrinkles galore, but she didn't bother mentioning it, or Maeve would probably pack an ironing board and iron as well!

Two hours later they'd significantly lightened Maeve's travel wardrobe. Maeve, frustrated, was near tears because she thought she should be taking much more. Charlotte, exasperated, couldn't get Maeve to understand that she *could* actually survive on even less.

"Really, Char! I don't know how you managed to travel all over the world," Maeve complained. "You might not know this, but I have a really hard time throwing fashion out the window. This is terrible! I'm going to be a disaster in front of all those models and designers in New York—I just know it!"

"I promise, they won't even notice your clothes," Charlotte assured. "They'll be way too wrapped up in the show and how they look. When you're lugging this stuff up and down the streets of Manhattan, you'll be *thanking* me. If you had let me do the packing, I bet I could have gotten everything into one bag!"

Maeve looked horrified. "No girl with any fashion sense could get it all in one bag!" she insisted. "Do you hear me? I have two words for you, Char—*NOT POSSIBLE!*"

A Gift from Kelley

Another Beacon Street Girl with more fashion sense than she knew what to do with *had* managed to get it all into one bag. Katani carefully checked off the last item on her list and inspected her neatly folded wardrobe. She was just about to close her black carry-on suitcase, confident that she had plenty of clothes for the weekend, but she counted off her list one more time: Two pairs of pants, her favorite jeans, and some vintage striped trousers (in case Michelle had the energy to take them out for dinner). Everything had been neatly ironed and folded. Katani packed three shirts that matched both pants and four scarves she'd hand-painted herself to dress them up. She'd rolled the scarves in fresh tissue paper, so they'd stay wrinkle-free in her suitcase.

She decided on two pairs of comfortable shoes, ankle socks, pajamas and underwear, plus some jewelry and scarves for accessorizing. She could wear her heavy duffle coat in the car. Katani also had plenty of toiletries and they were all practical, travel-sized bottles. She'd also remembered a travel alarm clock.

"More than enough," she said out loud. She zipped the bag shut, wiped her hands together, and breathed a sigh of relief. She was finally finished packing.

"Hi Katani!" Kelley shouted, bouncing into their room.

Ever since their parents had agreed to let Katani go to New York, Kelley had barely left Katani's side. She always seemed to be there, asking if Katani would play checkers with her, watch TV with her, or read to her before bed. Katani knew Kelley was getting more and more worried about her going away. She had tried to be soothing, saying she'd be home very soon, but Kelley wouldn't have it. She didn't want Katani leaving, period!

❀

Also, because Kelley was so anxious about Katani's trip, she tended to be louder and more boisterous than usual. But Katani refused to get upset with her. The mere idea of being mad at Kelley made Katani feel terrible. Though Kelley could be annoying, she loved Katani unconditionally, and Katani loved Kelley just as much.

"Hi Kelley," Katani replied to the enthusiastic greeting. She hoped Kelley wouldn't ask about her suitcase.

But Kelley noticed it right away. "What's in that, Katani? Is it something very beautiful and luscious?" Kelley loved to repeat the words she heard in TV commercials.

"Not luscious," Katani answered. "They're just some of my clothes. You know. Jeans and stuff."

"Why did you put them in the case?" Kelley asked, crossing her arms and giving Katani her *I'm smarter than you think* look. "They're supposed to go in your drawers."

Katani hesitated. "Well ... I put them in the case so I could carry them. For when I go to New York City." She hoped if she kept her answer low-key, it wouldn't upset Kelley.

Kelley looked at her for a long moment, and then her dark eyes started to fill up.

"Oh, Kelley!" Katani said, coming close to hug her. To her relief, Kelley let her. "It's OK! I'm going to find some luscious things to bring home to you, and we can play with them together, all right? It'll be so much fun!"

Kelley still stood a little stiffly. Her eyes were wet, but she managed to sniffle and ask, "What kind of luscious?"

"Well—uh—" Katani thought for a minute. "I don't know yet. What would you like?"

Solemnly, Kelley said, "Do they have luscious horses in New York City?"

That wasn't exactly the question that Katani expected.

She remembered one of Maeve's favorite movies set in New York in which people rode in a horse-drawn carriage around Central Park. "Yes, I think so …" Katani answered slowly. She knew what would be coming next.

"Then I want you to bring home a beautiful, luscious horse," Kelley said seriously. "I want it to be purple."

Katani cracked up. "I will!" she agreed, laughing. "I'll bring you the most luscious horse in New York City, OK? It isn't going to be a real horse, but I promise it'll be beautiful all the same. I'm not going to tell you what color though. It'll be a surprise."

Kelley wasn't laughing. She studied Katani for a moment, and then she straightened up and announced proudly, "I have a surprise for *you*, Miss Bossy!"

Kelley bolted over to her bed and started rummaging around. The space at the head of Kelley's bed was filled with her treasures—stuffed animals, favorite books, and lots of pictures and special projects she'd made in her art therapy classes. It was crammed with so much junk that Katani wondered how Kelley could find anything.

Once Kelley finally spotted what she was looking for, she bent way over the headboard and made a mighty snort to retrieve something. Then she turned around and skipped back to Katani.

"Here's the beautiful luscious horse that I made, Katani," she said with an outstretched hand. "It's for you."

It was a crude-looking ceramic pin in a garish gold color. It had taken Kelley almost a week to mold into a horse, and then she'd painted it bright gold. The horse had black eyes and a white mane, but it was mostly the strange shade of gold that made it stand out a mile. Kelley had chattered about it for hours when she first brought it home. She was extremely proud of it.

"Take him to New York, Katani," she said. "If I can't go with you, my horse can. Take care of him and wear him every day, OK?"

Katani gulped. For such a fashion-consious girl, she cringed at the thought of wearing a homemade clay pin—especially in the high fashion world of New York! But it was Kelley's gift to her, she reminded herself. This was Kelley's way of showing her love, and it meant a lot to Katani. Some things were just more important than fashion.

Katani tenderly cupped the pin in her hand. "Oh Kelley," she said. "He's beautiful. I promise I will wear him every day."

"I know," Kelley replied, "Because he's a beautiful, luscious horse."

CHAPTER 7

ভ

ON THE ROAD

"ISN'T THIS JUST A BEAUTIFUL DRIVE, GIRLS?" Mr. Taylor asked happily. Actually, Maeve thought, it was a lovely way to travel to New York. A crisp breeze and blue sunny sky made for a perfect Thursday afternoon. The majestic maple trees gracefully arched over the Merritt Parkway. Their autumn leaves, brilliant in bold shades of red and gold, rustled gently in the wind.

Everything outside the car is so pretty, Katani thought. "Katani … listen to this," Maeve said as she tugged on her arm. Maeve was in the middle of telling another story of a movie she'd seen at the Movie House, in between Sam spouting off World War II facts. Katani looked down at her sketchbook, hoping that Maeve would get the clue that she needed a little quiet time. No such luck. They were only an hour out of Brookline. One or all of the Kaplan-Taylors was always talking. The constant chatter was giving her a headache.

"Isn't this route fantastic, girls? Just look at this scenery!" Mr. Taylor marveled, interrupting his daughter in mid-sentence as she described in detail the final dance sequence in some Fred Astaire and Ginger Rogers movie (she couldn't remember which one). Finally, Katani, who had been doodling fashion designs in her sketchbook, began keeping a chart on the bottom of the page. She made a checkmark for every movie Maeve discussed, an X-mark for each of Sam's war facts, and a little star for every time Mr. Taylor said how wonderful the drive was. Mr. Taylor was way in the lead, twelve to five.

He continued, "The Merritt Parkway is famous. Did you know that the Merritt has 68 bridges? Each one is different, but they were all designed by the same person, George Dunkelberger. The Merritt Parkway is such a refreshing change from the new multilane interstates. Those roads have no character at all. Just big white concrete ribbons with ugly barriers. And they're crowded, too. Full of people anxious to get from Point A to Point B as quickly as possible. Not like this old road, no—siree! Now, this is *driving*! By the time you get where you're going, you feel truly alive! Why, I feel a song coming on! Come on! Everybody! *Ohhhh* what a beautiful morning ..."

Katani glanced at Maeve who, stifling a giggle, mouthed back, "He's not usually this bad."

"Sing with me, guys. Maeve, I *know* you know this one."

Maeve shrugged her shoulders, rolled her eyes at Katani and said, "If you can't beat 'em, join 'em!" Katani was aghast. Maeve's voice grew louder and was soon followed by Sam's squeaky off-key squawk. Katani was beginning to feel carsick. She had never seen Maeve's father act like this before! But boy was it clear from where Maeve inherited all her dramatic qualities.

Something about this wide open space must bring out the kid in Mr. Taylor. Not only had he been extolling the joys of the Merritt all day, singing as though he were the leader of a band, he also mentioned wanting to stop and have dinner with a college friend in Westport, Connecticut. Katani normally wouldn't mind, but she knew this addition to their itinerary would delay their arrival in New York by several hours, and she was eager to get to Michelle's apartment in Greenwich Village and chill out. Maybe she could lock herself in the bathroom and take a ten-minute hot shower.

Katani remembered from math class that the shortest distance between two points was a straight line. The old Merritt was far from straight, and it was narrow. The direct route was the interstate, which Mr. Taylor had already deemed abominable. So they were winding, looping, and zigzagging above, around, and under the direct route instead. They had been puttering in this manner for over four hours, and if Katani was reading the road signs correctly, it was at least another fifty miles to Westport. Katani thought Connecticut was as small as Massachusetts, but this drive was taking forever!

When Mr. Taylor ended his song, Maeve resumed another movie commentary, completely unfazed. "So then the little boy—I think his name is Sam—no, wait, that's Tom Hanks' name in the movie—the son's name is Josh—no, Jonah! That's it, Jonah. Anyhow, Jonah writes a letter to Meg Ryan *pretending to be the dad* and says he'd really like to meet her at the top of the Empire State Building on Valentine's Day, just like in *An Affair to Remember*!" Maeve sighed and clutched her heart. "It's all dreadfully romantic."

At this rate, Katani thought, it will probably be Valentine's Day by the time we actually get there! Katani really wanted to get to Greenwich Village at a decent hour because she and Maeve had to wake up super early in the morning to start working with Michelle. Oh well. There was

✿

nothing she could do about it now. She would just have to zen out. It was pretty obvious that Maeve and her dad were not going to stop talking any time soon, and Sam, who was only eight, was too excited to sit still. Katani had to admit Sam was pretty smart for his age. He piped in with the funniest things sometimes.

Just then Sam popped around his seat and turned to look at the girls in the back. "You know," he said gravely, "We could be going at light speed on a real highway! I think this curvy road is MALARKY." Katani couldn't help but giggle. Where did that boy come up with these things? "They're so much more fun to drive. Pleeeeease! It's not too late, Dad," he begged.

"What's the rush, Sam?" his father asked, smiling. "I'm sure Katani and Maeve would like to get to Greenwich Village, and I want to have that dinner with my friend in Westport. You have absolutely nothing to worry about. We're just going to stay on the good old Merritt, and we'll get to New York in plenty of time!"

Take a deep breath, Katani told herself then added silently, *OK, I'm not going to stress out any more. I am just going to think about New York*. She closed her eyes for a moment.

"Hey!" Maeve nudged her and held up a plastic bag full of apple slices. Yuri, the man who ran the market not too far from school, had given them to her that morning. Maeve announced that free apples were definitely a good omen for the trip. When she wasn't talking, she was crunching. "Try one, they're really delicious ... get it ... delicious apple!" Maeve handed Katani a slice, then laughed at her play on words.

Katani tried to smile as she took a bite. "Mmm! They are good." It not only tasted sweet, juicy, and crisp, but it made her feel a little better.

This wasn't so bad. Surely she could put up with a little

extra chatter. After all, if it hadn't been for Maeve, she never would have been on this trip in the first place. *If I can handle a fashion show, I can certainly handle this,* Katani thought to herself. Maybe it was just being in such tight quarters. Yes, that must be it, reasoned Katani. Kelley was a chatterbox too. She would just have to relax. And she really didn't want to seem ungrateful.

Just then the car hit a pothole and lurched to the side. "Uh-oh!" Mr. Taylor exclaimed.

"Uh-oh? What's 'Uh-oh?'" Maeve asked.

Katani could feel her heart pounding. Relaxing would just have to wait.

Mr. Taylor pulled hard on the steering wheel and frowned. "This is not good."

"What's wrong?" Katani gulped. Mr. Taylor was slowing down and pulling over to an upcoming exit. He stopped alongside a two-lane country road that made the Merritt look like an eight-lane superhighway. *Now I know what they mean by the middle of nowhere,* thought Katani.

Mr. Taylor got out of the station wagon and inspected the car on all sides. Suddenly his face appeared tap-tap-tapping at Maeve's window. Maeve cranked it open and her father announced, "Just as I thought, girls. We have a flat."

Katani couldn't believe it. Would they ever get to Greenwich Village?

"It's like the Wicked Witch of the West is following us all the way to Oz," Maeve commented in a low voice. Katani couldn't help laughing. It did feel like there was some force out there making sure they would be late.

Mr. Taylor popped open the trunk. "What's he doing?" Katani asked.

Maeve shrugged. "Changing the tire, I guess." She

✿

sighed. "Too bad he doesn't have the other car. This is our old car. The tools are kind of old-fashioned. My mom got the nice car so she could drive to Vermont to visit her old roommate—my father didn't want her to worry about anything happening ..." Her voice trailed off.

Katani wasn't sure what to say, so she touched Maeve's shoulder. She knew Maeve still felt terrible about her parents' separation and she wished she could do something to make her feel better.

Sam got out of the car to watch his father work on the tire and Katani and Maeve followed suit. Mr. Taylor reached into the trunk, shuffled some things around, and wrapped his arms around the tire. But as he started to lift it, he staggered a little and grabbed his back. The big round tire thudded back into the trunk, as Mr. Taylor sank to ground moaning.

Sam ran over and knelt beside him. "Dad? Hey, Dad, are you OK?!"

With a moan, Mr. Taylor pointed to his lower back.

"Oh, no!" Maeve cried. "He must have pulled a muscle! He has trouble with his back."

"Oh brother!" Sam squeaked worriedly.

"Is he going to be OK?" Katani asked. She wanted to bury her head in her arms and cry, but she knew that it certainly wouldn't help the situation.

Mr. Taylor was lying on the ground. He had one hand pressed into his back, and his face was contorted in a pained grimace. "OK, Dad, don't move," Maeve said quickly. She looked helplessly at Katani, who always seemed to know what to do in a crisis.

Katani, however, just shook her head. "I don't know how to change a tire!" she said.

Maeve looked petrified. "Well I don't know how either!"

Katani stared at her friend. *Be cool, Kgirl*, she reminded herself. She knelt down by Maeve's dad. "Mr. Taylor, are you OK?" she asked.

He nodded. "My back. You bend the wrong way—and it's all over!" He tried to laugh but it was just too painful.

Katani tried to stay calm. She didn't have any special CPR or emergency training, but she knew in an emergency you had to stay calm. She continued, "What do you usually do for it?"

"A little aspirin usually does the trick … and some ice."

"Do you know where the aspirin is?" Katani asked, preparing to break open suitcases to find it.

"I'll look in the glove compartment," volunteered Maeve.

He shook his head. "I don't think I have any with me."

Katani rolled her eyes. "Umm," she said, wracking her brain. "Let's call somebody! Yes, that's it, we can call somebody! Where's your cell phone?"

Sam looked at Maeve. Maeve looked at her father. Her father looked even more uncomfortable. "In my jacket, I think," he told her.

Katani retrieved his jacket from the front seat. She checked the pockets and the inside flaps. Nothing.

"Try the pocket on my brown suitcase," Mr. Taylor suggested weakly.

Katani quickly unzipped it. Lots of socks—no cell phone.

"Did I forget it?" he wondered. "*That* would have been a HUGE mistake."

The girls warily looked at each other. "Never mind, Dad," Maeve said. She tucked her dad's jacket under his head so he could lie more comfortably on the ground. It was not likely that's he'd be moving anytime soon. Every time he tried to get up he winced and had to lie back down.

Katani whipped out her business notebook and made a quick note: *Ask Mom and Dad to buy me a cell phone for emergency situations.* She wondered how long they'd have to wait there before Mr. Taylor would feel well enough to sit up. And what if he didn't feel well enough to drive? They could spend the whole weekend stuck out here in the middle of Nowheresville!

Sam seemed to be reading her mind. "Hey, no problem. I can change that tire in nothing flat," he boasted. "The first thing I need is an assistant." He looked at the girls and stuck out his hand. "WRENCH!" he called. Sam began to pry at the hubcap until his father noticed what was going on.

"Sam," Mr. Taylor said sharply. "Sam, step away from the hubcap. Just give me a few minutes kids. I'll be fine," he said after seeing the worried looks on everyone's faces.

Maeve and Katani looked at each other helplessly. "What do we know?" Maeve asked in a low voice.

Katani shook her head. "I don't have a clue. We've only gotten a flat tire once, and when we did, my dad was there to fix it."

"I can't believe this!" Maeve said quietly to Katani. "I'm sorry this trip is taking so long. If I were you, I'd be really bummed out," she added, looking genuinely miserable.

"Hey, it's OK," Katani said, trying to convince Maeve AND herself that it was. "These things happen, right?" She couldn't help but wonder how they were going to get out of this mess. They had phone, no idea where they were, no chance that another car would pass by, and the only adult in their group was lying on the ground in agony while his 8-year-old son tried to figure out how to change a tire.

Perfect.

"Wait a minute!" Mr. Taylor said suddenly. He tried to raise himself up, but that brought another groan. Still, he looked optimistic as he smacked his forehead. "Of course! I just remembered—I put the cell phone in the console underneath the arm rest!"

"Great!" clapped Maeve. She crawled into the front seat and popped open the middle arm rest to find everything— maps, a little flashlight, car registration, insurance information, and underneath the mass of paper—a small silver cell phone.

"Yes!" she breathed excitedly. She turned it on and handed it to her father. "Here you go!"

"Thanks, sweetheart." Fortunately, he had programmed his auto club emergency number into the phone. In under a minute he was in touch with someone from the AAA hotline. When he hung up, he announced that they were sending out a truck with someone to change the tire in about twenty minutes.

Maeve and Katani smiled at each other. Things were definitely looking up.

After fifteen minutes, Katani shivered and noticed that she could not longer see the exit sign in the distance. On the horizon, the sun was casting its last glimmer of gold. And through the magenta clouds, the pale moon was beginning to peek out.

"Look!" Katani said, pointing at the beautiful country sunset. She couldn't believe the day had ended so soon. They'd left Brookline in the early afternoon, and here it was already getting dark! "Where is daylight savings time when you really need it?" Katani whispered to Maeve.

Maeve cupped her ear. "Listen!" she said. There was a soft hooting that sounded like it came from the trees just behind them.

"Owls!" Sam said excitedly.

"Oh, no," Katani moaned. She liked some things about the nighttime, but creepy noises were not among them.

Looking at the stars was pleasant; imagining big birds of prey that hovered all around in the darkness was not!

Behind them, Mr. Taylor talked softly on his cell phone. "That's right, Larry," he said. "It's been a rough day, and we're temporarily stranded ... Well, no ... Thanks for the offer, but we can't stay with you ... I've got to get my daughter and her friend to New York City, and hopefully tonight ... Yup, I'm sure we'll do it another time soon ... Sure thing, Larry ... Thanks for being so understanding."

He clicked off the phone and smiled cheerfully at Katani. "Well, this is quite an adventure!"

Katani tried to smile at him. She also knew lots of people who thought outdoor adventures were great, who liked dealing with challenges and problems. Katani Summers was not a nature lover, and furthermore, she'd already overcome a ton of problems just last week. And for what? To end up stranded in the middle of nowhere in the dark with a hooting owl, an injured man, and a crippled vehicle? *Adventure*, Katani thought dismally to herself, *was definitely overrated. Give me fashion any day*!

CHAPTER 8

❦

SALLY TO THE RESCUE

TEN MINUTES CRAWLED BY, though to the stranded travelers it felt like an hour. The night sounds grew louder, as Mr. Taylor managed to lower himself into a comfortable position without groaning. Maeve and Katani looked nervously at each other. This was not fun. Would Mr. Taylor ever be able to drive?

Then suddenly, they heard a sound that made them all hopeful. It was the low rumble of a car.

Even better—it was a state trooper's car!

"Look!" Katani cried. She threw up her arms and shouted, "Stop. Please stop!"

The car slowed down and pulled to a stop behind them.

"Oh, sweet!" Sam exclaimed. "Whoa, a state trooper! Awesome! This is almost as cool as meeting an army dude!"

"Sam, stop trying to sound like you're a teenager," an annoyed Maeve snapped at her brother.

Ignoring his sister, Sam dropped his jack on the ground and dashed over to meet the trooper. The trooper was a tall, young man who drove a beige cruiser with flashing lights.

The trooper got out of his car and sauntered over to Mr. Ramsey, who was on the grass. He was clad in full uniform with a brimmed black hat, shiny black boots, and a black leather belt. "Wait 'til I tell Harry!" Sam murmured under his breath when he saw the shiny gleam of the trooper's pistol resting safely in the holster.

"What seems to be the trouble here?" the trooper asked. No one answered for a minute. Mr. Taylor strained to sit up and actually made it this time.

Sam straightened to his fullest height, which at eight years old wasn't all that impressive, and whipped his hand sharply to his brow. "We have the situation under control, sir," he barked. Sam gave him a fierce salute and added, "You can go back to your duties now."

The trooper raised an eyebrow. "Oh, really?" he remarked, looking at the flat tire and the stricken Mr. Taylor. "Well, maybe I can still be of some help."

He started toward Mr. Taylor. "He's so handsome!" Maeve whispered to Katani. Katani hadn't even noticed. She was just thrilled that ever since they had been discovered, the creepy night sounds seemed to have vanished.

The trooper squatted by Mr. Taylor. "What happened here, sir?" he asked. Mr. Taylor explained how he'd tried to lift out the spare tire and had thrown his back out. The trooper nodded. "I have some Advil and some ice in the cruiser. Would that help?"

Mr. Taylor looked relieved. "Yes, a lot!"

"You're our hero!" Maeve blurted out. Katani gave her a look as the trooper turned. "What?" Maeve asked Katani, who rolled her eyes.

The trooper passed Sam, who was still standing stiffly at attention "At ease," the trooper said with a wink after he snapped off a smart-looking counter salute. Sam sighed and brought his hand to his side.

"Here you go," the trooper said. He handed Mr. Taylor a first-aid sample packet of two Advil pills along with an ice pack. "I've pulled my back before," he said. "The ice and Advil really does the trick. Give it about ten minutes."

Just then, they all heard the screech of tires. "Gee, it's getting a lot busier on this road," Maeve said to Katani.

"Yeah! Two more cars ... we're very popular," Katani said. Her heart lifted when she saw that it was a tow truck. The words "Sally's Service Station" were painted on the side in blue letters. *That's pretty cool*, she thought, *a service station with a girl's name!*

The young woman who jumped down from the truck looked like a Hollywood movie version of a garage mechanic. She was slender and blue-eyed, and her light blonde hair was pulled back in a ponytail. Katani noticed that she was wearing some kind of jumpsuit, though it was hard to make out much as the darkness was thickening around them. "Hi, I'm Sally," she said. "Triple-A sent me to fix your flat."

There was something quite impressive about this Sally woman, Maeve thought to herself. She couldn't be more than five foot three, and yet here she was, striding confidently over to the front of the car, assessing the situation in a couple of swift glances. She looked at Mr. Taylor recovering on the ground, the state trooper, and Sam, who was inspecting the flat. "You girls must have had a very, um, exciting day ..." Sally said, giving the girls a sympathetic smile as she went back to her truck.

Sam offered her the jack he had been playing with, but she declined, saying kindly, "You've got good tools there, but I do better with my own." She brought back an assortment of objects, including an industrial-size flashlight, and placed them within easy reach by the flat tire, clicking on the flashlight so it illuminated the entire area. The girls drew closer to her like moths to a flame. "So do you guys know much about car maintenance?" Sally asked. From the baffled looks on Maeve and Katani's faces she concluded, "I guess that's a no!"

"I don't know the first thing about changing a tire!" Maeve admitted and Katani nodded in agreement.

"I'll let you in on a little secret: it's not as hard as it looks. Watch, I'll show you," Sally declared. She looked at the tire. "I see someone tried to get the hubcap off."

"That was Sam," Maeve said proudly.

"The hubcap is the cover on the wheel, and sometimes it's got kind of a sporty design. You've heard people talking about stolen hubcaps?" asked Sally.

"Well, in movies," Maeve said, exchanging glances with Katani. Katani nodded. The amount of stuff Maeve learned from movies was incredible.

"Well, hubcaps sometimes do get stolen in real life," Sally said. "People steal them because they can sell them to someone else with a totally different car and the hubcap will still fit. Also people with sporty cars like to have sporty covers on their wheels to match, so there's a big market for them."

"Is it sort of like the different covers you put on cell phones?" Maeve asked, thinking of her own pink, sparkly cover on the phone she'd mistakenly left at home.

Sally nodded vigorously. "Exactly!"

"Oh, I get it," Katani said, surprised that she really did understand. Sally explained things so simply, and at the same time she treated the girls as if they were her equals. It made it easy to learn from her.

Sally carefully laid the hubcap down a few feet away and

said, "First, the jack." She swiftly stuck the jack in back of the flat tire and began to pump it up.

When she saw the girls' puzzled looks, she explained, "We have to lift the car up in order to change the tire. That's what the jack does. You just put it in the same area as the flat but far enough away so it doesn't interfere with your changing the tire. Then pump it up!"

She pumped vigorously, and in a few minutes the jack was holding the car aloft. "Now, the lug nuts." Sally showed them some small, shiny, nut-like objects around the edge of the tire. "They keep the tire securely attached to the car," she said. "Take these bad boys off and you can get that tire off in no time at all!" Sam hovered closely.

She whipped off the lug nuts and placed them inside the hubcap for safekeeping. "Hey dude," Sally nodded to Sam. "Keep an eye on these, pal. We don't want them rolling away." Sam was thrilled to be given a job.

Katani was fascinated as she watched Sally work. Maeve was captivated as well. The way that Sally demonstrated how to change the tire really made it seem possible! *OK*, Katani thought. *I think I could do that!*

Maeve broke away from Sally to see how her father was doing. The trooper had helped Mr. Taylor sit up. His face had a lot more color now, and he hadn't made a single groan since he'd put the ice pack on his back. "Hey, Dad, you look better!" she called. Things were improving.

"I *feel* better, honey," her father called back. "The Advil and ice really did the trick! I think I can drive again as soon as the tire is ready."

"I'm glad to hear it," the trooper declared. "You think you could stand up and stretch a little? Might help even more."

Mr. Taylor seemed agreeable, so the trooper helped him

up. With one last mighty, "Uuuuuughhhh!" Mr. Taylor struggled to his feet.

"Yay Dad!" Sam cheered.

Maeve turned back, smiling, to Sally. "Dad was in bad shape there until the trooper showed up." She stole a glance at the handsome trooper, who reminded her of Brad Pitt, then turned her attention back to the tire.

Sally agreed, "Well that's one of the reasons we have state troopers. To help travelers in need, right? OK, we're almost done." She quickly shifted the flat tire off the wheel and replaced it with the spare. "Who put the spare over here?" she said with a smile.

"That was me," Sam said, coming over to watch her. There was a hint of pride in his face.

"Well done," Sally told him. "You put the spare right where a mechanic could easily reach it. Nice going."

Maeve and Katani looked at each other. They decided not to embarrass Sam by pointing out that putting the spare on the ground was about as far as he could get in figuring out how to change the tire!

Sally was right … there really was nothing to it. The new tire was ready to go in no time. Sally placed the lug nuts in their proper position, but she didn't tighten them all the way. "Just remember to put them on in a star pattern. And don't tighten them all the way until you've let down the jack."

Once Sally had gently let down the jack and removed it, she used a small hand drill to tighten the lug nuts all the way. She replaced the wheel cover and wiped her hands on her denim jumpsuit.

"Finished!" she announced.

"That's it?" Maeve couldn't believe it. "I always thought cars were so complicated—my mother complains about them all the time!"

"It's really not that bad once you get the hang of it," Sally reassured her. "In fact, you can take classes that'll teach you stuff like this. You can learn how to change tires and change oil, and how to do simple maintenance on your car ... that kind of thing. Let me tell you, girls, the secret to a happy life is to to do what you are most interested in and to learn about the practical things too, like car maintenance. You'll feel very independent. I took a class like that in high school and ended up rebuilding an old Volkswagen Bug I found in a junkyard. Drove it for three years, too. Boy, oh, boy, was the rest of my class jealous!"

"That's a great idea," Katani said to her. "I'd like to run my own business someday, and I hate the idea of being dependent on other people to do things I should know how to do myself."

Sally picked up her tools and looked appraisingly at Katani. "Good attitude! Being empowered—that's the ticket."

"I can't believe how far we still have to go tonight!" Maeve said with a laugh, looking a lot more cheerful now that her father was feeling better and the car was fixed.

"Well, it looks like my work here is done!" Sally declared with a big smile. Maeve almost burst out laughing. Sam was dreamily staring at Sally!

The trooper was ready to leave too. "Take this extra packet of Advil with you, just in case," he told Mr. Taylor.

Sally organized her paperwork while the trooper made sure that Mr. Taylor was comfortable walking around by himself. "Thanks so much, officer. And you too, Sally. You two were real lifesavers today!" Mr. Taylor said gratefully.

"You can say that again!" Katani mumbled softly.

Sally took a clipboard over to Mr. Taylor. "All you need to do is sign here, and I'll be on my way," she said, handing

Mr. Taylor the AAA form.

The trooper gave Sam a final salute and then turned to the girls. "You two, watch out for this guy," he instructed, tilting his head at Maeve's dad. "Make sure he doesn't do any more heavy lifting!"

"Don't worry," Sally called as she got into her truck. "If they get another flat, I think these ladies will be able to handle it!"

The girls laughed and waved good-bye to Sally and to the trooper.

Mr. Taylor restarted the car, and Maeve and Katani felt a wave of relief as they finally pulled onto the road again. "That trooper was soooo dreamy!" Maeve whispered to Katani.

Katani nodded. "Sally was way cool too," she added. "I feel like telling my grandmother to start a car maintenance class at school. I mean, how can you really be independent if you don't even know what to do when your car breaks down?"

"I don't know," Maeve said. "It sounds great, but," she glanced down at her soft, pink sweater, "angora-wool blends really don't match with car grease."

"Well, someday I am going to take a class like that," Katani declared. "I never want to be stuck by the side of the road again!" She dug out the notebook she kept for business ideas and carefully noted down Sally's suggestion. That one was a keeper!

CHAPTER 9

ℭ

IF I CAN MAKE IT THERE ...

IT WAS ALMOST 11 O'CLOCK and completely dark by the time the Taylors' station wagon reached the streets of Greenwich Village in New York City. "We should be right around the corner," Maeve whispered reassuringly to Katani. "I can't wait. I'm so tired I could fall asleep right here!" True to her word, in about a minute Maeve had completely dozed off. Sam had been asleep since they left Connecticut.

"What's the address again, Katani?" Mr. Taylor called.

Katani looked at the directions her mother had written down. "It's on Morton Street, just off of Houston Street," Katani told him. "I think it's about five minutes away." She read the address out again, but it took more than five minutes for Mr. Taylor to negotiate the streets. Twenty minutes went by, and she realized they were good and lost. To make matters worse, it was getting really late. If they didn't get to Michelle's soon, she would be too exhausted to do anything in the morning!

"Katani?" Mr. Taylor asked, taking out his cell phone. "Would you mind calling Michelle and asking for more specific directions? I am not really familiar with the Village."

He handed Katani the phone and she punched in her cousin's numbers.

"Michelle?" she said when her cousin answered sleepily. "It's Katani. We're driving around the Village right now and we can't find your street."

Michelle let out a giant yawn and answered, "That's the problem with my neighborhood. The entire rest of Manhattan is a numbered grid, so it's hard to get lost there. But, not the Village!"

"I can see that … OK I am going to give the phone to Maeve's dad so you can tell him where to go," Katani said as she handed the phone back to Mr. Taylor.

Michelle was right. The streets seemed to be some kind of paved over cow paths, thought Katani. Michelle kept asking them to give her cross streets so she could "locate" them. After ten more minutes of cruising aimlessly, Mr. Taylor had an idea. "Thanks for all your help, Michelle. We should be there soon," he said and hung up.

"Did you figure it out?" Katani asked.

"Not really," he answered. "But I have an idea …" Mr. Taylor pulled the car to the side of the street right in front of the bright lights and open windows of a Korean deli. "The only way we are going to find her place is by asking a person to point out the way. Now Katani, since these two are out like a light, would you mind hopping out and just asking the clerk for directions to Morton Street? I can keep an eye on you from right here."

"Sure." Katani got out and walked inside the brightly lit store. She had heard that New York was famous for its delis and now she knew why. The air was rich with the smell of cured meat and spices. There was an elderly man working at the cash register and a woman stocking the shelves. The man looked up at the sound of the bell that rang when Katani walked in. "Excuse me," she said in a friendly tone, "we just came in from Boston and we're kind of lost. We're trying to find Morton Street, but we keep missing it."

She showed the man Michelle's address neatly written in her business idea notebook.

The clerk looked at her as though she were crazy, and pointed behind her.

"What?" Katani asked.

"One block away. You turn right at this corner, you're there." He waved his hands at her.

"Are you serious?" Katani asked. After all this time driving around, they were only one block away from Michelle's house?

"Yes. Yes, that's it." The clerk smiled at her thunderstruck expression. "Have a good evening."

Katani smiled gratefully at him. "You too! Thanks."

Five minutes later, they were in front of Michelle's apartment building. When they told the doorman their names, he gallantly held the door open and said comfortingly, "Ah yes, Michelle is expecting you." Sam helped Maeve lug in her two enormous suitcases. Katani managed just fine with her small black carry-on bag.

Once in Michelle's building, Maeve was eager to be on her own. "Thanks, Dad. Thanks, Sam," she said. "I think we're all set here. "See you Sunday! I'll call you. *Ciao!*" Katani snorted. Maeve loved to pretend she was in a foreign movie. Tonight she was in her Italian mode.

"Hold your horses, young lady," her father said. "I'm not leaving until Katani's cousin comes down to meet you."

"But Daaaaad ... We're not eight!" Maeve whined. She looked at Sam, who was sleepily slumped on a bench against the wall beside them.

"I don't care if you're twenty-eight. I'm your father, and I will be waiting!" He raised his eyebrow which Maeve knew was his sign that he meant business.

At first, Katani thought that Mr. Taylor was being a little overprotective. Then again, after everything else that had happened today, waiting for Michelle was probably not a bad idea! She used Mr. Taylor's cell phone to call Michelle and ask her to come down.

Two minutes later, Michelle, in fluffy slippers and a yellow bathrobe tied hastily around her, shuffled off the elevator. As always, she was smiling. "Hi, everyone! You must be Maeve of the famous Beacon Street Girls. Katani's told me so much about you!" she said. Maeve glowed. "And you must be Mr. Taylor. Thanks so much for bringing them."

"It was no trouble at all," he said, winking at the girls. Maeve and Katani gave each other a look. No trouble? "Maeve, take my cell phone. In case of emergencies, call your mom. And have a great time. I'll see you back here on Saturday." Mr. Taylor kissed Maeve on the forehead, collected Sam, and they were on their way.

"So how was the trip?" asked Michelle once they'd wrestled Maeve's suitcases into the elevator and were riding up. Katani looked at Maeve, who just giggled and said, "Oh it was … interesting." Maeve and Katani took turns telling Michelle all about the Merritt Parkway, the flat tire, Mr. Taylor's bad back, and Sam's funny but useless attempts to help.

Michelle listened attentively as she led them into her fifth-floor apartment. "Wow, look at this place. It's amazing!" Maeve gasped, breaking off in the middle of the story to stare around the huge room. With high, arching ceilings and big windows overlooking the Village, the apartment seemed absolutely enormous even though it was really quite small. There was even a fireplace at one end of the room that would light up by pressing a remote control. "Too cool!" Maeve whispered.

"It's sooo fabulous, Michelle," Katani enthused. Katani couldn't wait to have an apartment like this.

"Well I'm glad you like it. All right, girls, follow me. You're going to sleep in the study." Michelle led the way down the narrow hall and opened a door on the right. "The couch is a pullout bed, but it's really comfy. You can ask any of my girlfriends from college. Most of them have spent a night at Hotel Michelle. You guys must be exhausted after your crazy trip, so if you want to go right to sleep that is A-OK by me—" She stopped and looked at them doubtfully. "Or do you want to eat something?"

"We stopped at a little diner back in Connecticut, so I'm all set," said Katani, "I think if I don't get into bed this minute, I'm going to sleep standing up."

Maeve nodded. "Me too. I've never been so tired in my whole life!" she said, collapsing on the fluffy coach.

"Sleep tight, girls." Michelle said as she turned off one of the lights and closed the door.

"Katani, this is the greatest place!" Maeve whispered. "And Michelle is awesome! She's so together, you know? I bet she can handle anything!"

Katani took off her coat and laid it carefully across an overstuffed chair in the corner. "She can. That's why she got promoted so quickly at *Teen Beat*. Everyone's really impressed with how professional she is."

Maeve strolled around the room, admiring Michelle's computer desk, the neat stacks of papers and files, and the rows of framed photographs of her and various celebrities on the walls. As Maeve walked, she dropped her jacket on the middle of the floor, kicked her pink boots against the wall, then unsnapped her favorite jeans and tossed them on a chair. Maeve put on her pjs and a minute later she lay diagonally on the pullout couch, sprawled over the blanket, and was fast asleep.

Katani stood frozen in dismay. She couldn't leave this study so messy, with Maeve's clothes lying all over the place like confetti! Michelle was as orderly as Katani, and would hate to see her once-meticulous study looking like a hurricane hit. Since Maeve was her friend, Katani herself felt responsible. After all, they were guests.

Slowly, she began to pick up Maeve's coat, boots, and jeans. She folded the clothes on a low table and neatly placed the boots underneath. Then she wearily took off her own clothes and put them back in her suitcase where they'd be out of Michelle's way.

Maeve was already sound asleep *on top of* the bed and blanket, so there was no way to make it up properly. Katani pulled a clean pillowcase over a fluffy pillow and crawled over Maeve, who had taken up most of the mattress. She wrapped herself in another blanket and squirmed around until she was finally comfortable.

Even though Katani was tired, she had a difficult time falling asleep. Too much had happened that day, and she needed to sort it all out in her mind. Maeve was so sweet and supportive. If it wasn't for Maeve, Katani never would have had the chance to go to New York in the first place. But Maeve could be so disorganized. *Charlotte and Isabel are always so much neater*, she thought. Would she have been better off bringing a different member of the BSG on her New York adventure? Maybe Maeve was just too tired to pick up after herself, Katani thought. Was this going to happen on the whole trip, or just tonight?

Katani tried to push those thoughts out of her mind as she finally drifted off to sleep. She and Maeve were awesome friends, and they were going to have a wonderful time. This trip would be the real start of her great career in business and fashion. She couldn't wait until tomorrow!

CHAPTER 10

&

THE MUSEUM LEECH

ON FRIDAY, THE ABIGAIL ADAMS seventh-grade class finished their second day of aptitude tests at precisely 11 o'clock. Ms. Rodriguez came back into the classroom with a smile. "All right, boys and girls. We're off to the Museum of Fine Arts!" Almost before Ms. R uttered her last syllable Dillon was out the door followed by the Trentinis and the Yurtmeister. They chanted "Field Trip! Field Trip!" all the way down the hall.

It was sunny outside under the high blue sky. "Perfect weather for a trip to a museum. Not! We should be going to the park for a class soccer game!" Avery exclaimed. She, Charlotte, and Isabel lined up in front of the bus that was waiting to take them to the museum.

Isabel shifted nervously from one foot to the other.

"What's wrong, Iz?" Charlotte asked.

Isabel shrugged. "Nothing really. I was just thinking about that test ... I don't know if I did that well on the math part. All the problems with X's and Y's really confused me. I don't think I got more than half of those!"

"I wouldn't worry too much," Charlotte reassured her. "Aptitude tests are just to see what you can and can't do. That way, school teachers know what they need to spend more time working on."

Avery was jumping to get to the front of the line, eager to obtain a choice seat on the bus. "Come on, can we *not* talk about tests anymore? This is supposed to be fun time!"

Isabel nodded. "I know, but that math …"

"Don't worry, Iz. I don't know if I did that great either," said Charlotte, hoping to reassure her friend.

"Isabel and Charlotte!" Avery interrupted, placing her hands on her hips. "Iz, do you want to be a famous artist or a math teacher?"

Isabel began to grin. "Well an artist but …"

"And Charlotte," Avery continued, "You *know* you are good at math and reading. You know more about astronomy than anyone at our school, and everybody loves reading your articles for *The Sentinel*."

"You're right," said Isabel. "I'll just have to wait to get the results and be surprised …"

"Speaking of surprises …" Avery motioned at a young woman walking toward the bus.

"Omigosh!" Charlotte said. "Look who's coming on the field trip with us!" She nodded at a young woman talking to Ms. Rodriguez.

"Ms. Weston!" Isabel exclaimed. "You don't think she's going to guide us around the museum, do you?"

"If she is, we might not make it home," Avery giggled. All three girls laughed, remembering their adventures at Lake Rescue with the directionally challenged student teacher, who couldn't seem to find her way around a parking lot, let alone the wilderness.

The bus ride to the museum seemed much shorter than it actually was. Everyone had way too much energy after being cooped up all morning taking tests. Now the bus was rocking with noise and laughter. "Hey, a truck! Let's get him to honk!" Henry Yurt yelled from his seat in the back. Nick and Dillon were ready for action. The three boys pumped their arms up and down as a Mac truck approached from the side. "Honk! Honk! Honk!" chanted the back of the bus. The driver took note of the squad of overexcited students and reached up and pulled down a lever.

"WONK! WONK!" bellowed the truck. It was more like the foghorn of a ship than a car. Some students covered their ears in surprise. The truck driver zoomed past and honked his horn one more time for good measure as he gave his bus of fans a friendly wave. The entire bus cheered loudly and waved back.

"I think I lost my hearing!" Isabel moaned as she clasped her hands over her ears.

Avery giggled and motioned toward Riley, who was sitting in front of them. Riley had headphones on and was bopping along to the tunes in his head, completely oblivious to the earth-shattering truck horn only moments before. "Hey Riley, how are the ear drums holding up?" Avery tapped his shoulder.

Riley, startled, pulled his earphones out and looked up. "What up?" Because he was part of a rock band called Mustard Monkey, most of the time there was some sort of loud musical noise blaring in his ears. "Are you talking to me?!" he asked in an overly loud voice.

"Never mind ..." Avery shook her head. She sat back next to Charlotte and began tapping her feet against the floor. After the morning-long test, Avery was just one of the many kids in Ms. Rodriguez' class who had a lot of leftover energy. "I wish we got to go on a field trip to a rock-climbing gym." Avery pretended to climb in place.

"Avery, this museum has mummies in crypts," Charlotte rubbed her hands to together gleefully.

Avery clapped. "Mummies! Now we're talking! Remember that scene in *Return of the Mummy* when ..."

Isabel shuddered. "I *really* don't want to see the mummies," she said sounding adamant.

"Why not, Izzy?" asked Charlotte.

"Yeah ... they've already been dead for about, I don't know, a thousand years," Avery said with a mischievous grin. "What do you think they're going to do, crawl out of their sarcophaguses and change their minds?"

Isabel tried to glare but giggled instead. "Ha ha, you are sooo funny, Avery." She reached under her seat and produced a straw handbag, which held a sketchbook and a box of colored pencils. "Oh well. I have plenty of stuff to do at the museum that will help me steer clear of mummies AND their sarcophaguses. There'll be some beautiful Egyptian art I can copy there. I've always thought Egyptian urns and murals were really cool. You know, the pictures on them all tell stories. I wouldn't mind just being by myself and sketching today. Am I the only seventh grader whose idea of an awesome day is looking at vases at a museum?"

"Umm ..." Avery began to drum her fingers together as she made a funny face at Isabel.

"No, no, no," Charlotte said quickly. "I'm excited too! I have a *Sentinel* assignment to work on today. Jennifer asked me to do a piece about our field trip for the paper."

"*You're* doing a piece for the paper?" The BSG turned around. Betsy Fitzgerald sat behind them, and now she was looking at Charlotte unhappily. "I wonder why Jennifer didn't ask me to write it? I told her that I am a real Egyptophile and I know everything about Egypt already. Remember I was telling you both about that really big essay contest I won in third grade when I wrote about the Pyramids?"

Charlotte shifted awkwardly in her seat. "Yes ..." she said, looking uncomfortable.

Betsy tossed her head. "If you want me to coauthor the piece, I'd be happy to help you. We wouldn't have to do any research because I've already got tons of information."

"Maybe it's not supposed to be all about facts and research, Betsy," Avery piped in. "The school paper is supposed to be about what's happening at school ... not just a list of boring facts."

Charlotte cringed. Avery could be so clueless sometimes.

Betsy shrunk back in her seat and whispered hopefully, "Well, if you change your mind ..."

"I'll definitely ask you if I need help on the historical parts," Charlotte offered with a smile. Betsy was one of those people who was so annoying but nice at the same time. Charlotte certainly didn't want to hurt her feelings.

"Hey, Izzy, maybe *The Sentinel* will use your sketches to illustrate Charlotte's article," Avery suggested.

"How cool would *that* be, Iz!" Charlotte said excitedly.

Isabel's rich brown eyes sparkled. "Oh, I'd love to have my drawings next to your article in *The Sentinel*!"

"Maybe," Avery murmured, "you can even draw a *pyramid*." She nudged Isabel, and the girls burst out laughing.

"No, maybe I'll even draw a mummy!" Isabel joked as she reached over and tugged Avery's hair.

Once the bus dropped them off at the entrance of Boston's famous Museum of Fine Arts, the teachers quickly organized students into groups based on who wanted to see what. Avery, Charlotte, and Isabel insisted on being in the same group. "After all," Avery said, "It doesn't really matter what we see, as long as we get to hang out together."

Ms. Rodriguez had split off a number of groups that had already moved off and started touring. "The rest of you will be with Ms. Weston and me," she said. The BSG turned around. There were four other girls in their group plus Ms. Weston with her happy smile. But the biggest surprise was the last member standing alone with his gigantic backpack. Danny Pellegrino shuffled over to the group and gave Isabel a wide grin. A museum docent, or tour guide, was waiting to escort them around.

Avery looked quickly at their group. "Figures, Danny's the only guy in our group," she said in a low voice to Charlotte and Isabel.

"Why do I think this is not an accident?" Charlotte asked.

"I think *someone* here wishes that our field trip was to the Isabel Martinez Museum instead," Avery whispered. Danny Pellegrino had been making moon eyes over Isabel for more than a week. He was driving her bonkers.

"Shh!" Isabel giggled.

"I think you're going to be very excited about our first stop today," said the guide as she led them down the stately museum hallways adorned with Flemish paintings. "We are headed toward the Mummy Room!" She ushered them around the corner.

"Yesssssss!" Avery hissed.

"Ugh," gulped Isabel. "I was hoping that the mummy

room would be at the very end so I could work up to it."

The entrance to the Mummy Room was designed like a tomb, with two thick columns covered with hieroglyphics. Isabel lingered by the columns while her classmates filtered into the room.

"Oooh, look at these!" Avery cried, rushing over to the wall where three or four mummy cases leaned. Each mummy had a card in front of it that explained who the person was inside.

Charlotte followed Avery, occasionally scribbling a thought down in her notebook. She was surprised to find that the information on the mummies was really interesting. Almost all of them were royalty or soldiers. Charlotte pointed to a smoothed stone statue with a face and headdress. It was huge—at least a foot taller than she was. A card explained that it was the lid of the sarcophagus of General Kheper-Re dating back between 570-526 B.C. The card also described the treasures that were buried with the mummies. The ancient Egyptians believed the spirits of the dead would use these treasures in their afterlife.

"Do you think the kids at Abigail Adams would be interested to know that Ancient Egyptians totally believed in life after death?" Charlotte asked Avery.

"Maybe," Avery shrugged, "But personally, I think you should write about how creepy these sarcophagus heads are. Check out this dude's eyes ... no eyeballs!"

Charlotte giggled and whispered, "And look at all the little hieroglyphics on it! There are worms, and people shooting bows and arrows. Oh, and look at all the tiny birds. Izzy would love these."

"Where is she anyway?" asked Avery as she turned around. Isabel had disappeared..

Anxious to avoid the mummies, Isabel had spotted a

small, elegant portrait, just outside the Mummy Room. *Phew! I'm safe,* she thought to herself.

There was something so familiar about the tiny painting. With the little brush strokes, pearly pink mouth, and soulful brown eyes, Isabel believed it looked like something she could have painted herself. The woman wore two necklaces: a string of emeralds, and a linked-gold chain. Isabel realized that she had seen jewelry like that in stores just the other day. She glanced at the card to see when this was painted. The card read "About A.D. 100." *This look certainly has made a comeback,* Isabel thought with a smile. Above the date the card also read "Fragmentary mummy portrait of a woman." This gave Isabel the shivers, but she dutifully took out her sketchbook and box of colored pencils and flipped open to a blank page. *Well, as long as I'm not* near *the mummies I'll be just fine!* And with a black pencil, she gracefully etched out the outlines of the woman's tiny ringlets and dainty cleft chin.

"Did you know that Ancient Egyptians *worshipped* cats," said a voice from behind her. "Did you know they even had cat mummies?"

Isabel, startled, dropped her pencil and just managed to catch her sketchbook before it fell to the ground. "Uugh … I didn't see you there," she muttered.

"Allow me," offered Danny Pellegrino, retrieving her pencil with a dramatic bow. "*Me lady.*" He presented the ordinary black pencil resting on his two hands as if it were the Hope Diamond.

"Um, thanks," was all Isabel could say.

"So where was I? Oh yeah! Cats. Did you see all the cats in their murals and the paintings of their houses? And did you know they had ceremonies when they mummified their dead cats?"

❁

"No, I did not know this." Isabel was trying to be polite but she craved time alone with her pencil and paper. She looked around for Betsy Fitzgerald. Maybe Betsy could channel Danny's Egyptian energies away from her.

Danny put one hand on his hip and the other on the glass case in a casual side-lean.

"Hands OFF the glass, please!" ordered a guard who was watching him carefully. Danny turned beet red, mumbled an apology, and stuffed both hands in his pockets.

This guy is a disaster! Isabel rolled her eyes. "Danny, you're going to get us *both* in trouble."

Danny barely skipped a beat as he moved quickly on with his lesson. "Did you know that Ancient Egyptians were buried with their cat mummies?"

Breathing deeply, Isabel clutched the sides of her notebook. This was going to be a trying day. "Well, actually, I'm not a big fan of mummies. Not even cat mummies," she muttered.

"I don't think this museum has cat mummies," Danny said. "Lemme check with the guide. You'll be here for a while? You're still working on your drawing, right?"

"Yeah," Isabel said. He could check on anything he wanted, as long as he'd just leave her alone!

"Phew! OK I'll be right back, don't worry." Danny scurried off like a man on a mission. The minute he walked away, Isabel hurried to another part of the room. If she couldn't sketch the portrait in peace, maybe she could copy this pretty painting of a pair of servants respectfully serving dinner to their master and mistress. The lines were graceful and elegant. Isabel thought this might even turn out better than the woman with the beautiful jewelry.

She had just flipped to a fresh sheet in her notebook when she heard, "I was right, Isabel. The guide says they don't have any cat mummies in the museum. That's a relief for you, huh? Now you can just draw away and you have nothing to worry about."

Danny was so proud of himself he looked like he was going to pop, thought Isabel. She had a sudden vision of Danny as a huge balloon floating in the air and spouting useless facts, shouting, "Vote for me!"

Isabel pressed her lips together tightly to prevent herself from screaming. "Mmm hmm," she nodded. Nothing to worry about? What would it take to get Danny to leave her in peace? He seemed, at least for the moment, to be completely absorbed in an amulet in a glass case. Maybe she could concentrate once more. As soon as she started a new drawing, Danny popped up and said with a hopeful smile, "¿Cómo estás?"

The only thing more annoying than Danny making small talk in English was Danny making small talk in Español. Could someone save her please? She looked around for Avery, who could send Danny away in a minute and wouldn't worry too much about hurting his feelings. Worrying about hurting someone's feelings could be a real burden sometimes, she thought.

"Did you know," he inquired, "that Egyptian women made sure they were buried with their cosmetics, too? They used tons of makeup every day. Did you know they were supposedly as beautiful as supermodels are today? Of course they weren't as beautiful as … well never mind."

Isabel groaned. "Danny, you are driving me crazy."

Once again, Danny had become magenta, but he couldn't stop himself from demonstrating his vast artillery of pointless facts. Now Danny was pointing to a small object in the case. He uttered a word and dramatically let the letters roll off his tongue. Isabel thought it sounded a little like Spanish—but

❀

not like any Spanish she'd ever heard before! Then he nudged her and pointed to another trinket and again said something with a strange, Spanish-like accent.

Danny must have been trying to say something in Spanish, but he wasn't even close. Isabel had been at the museum for almost an hour and she had barely made a scribble. If she didn't get away from Danny, she would never come up with a picture for Charlotte's article.

"Look," she said, throwing down her pencil, "Danny, no offense, but I don't even care about makeup all that much myself, and anyway, I'm not studying makeup today, or anything else! I am here to draw and I haven't gotten much done ..." As she waited for her words to sink in, she hoped she hadn't been too harsh. She gave him a quick smile. Big mistake!

Danny shook he was so happy. "Come on, Isabel," he continued. "Don't be so hard on yourself," Danny wasn't trying to leave her alone ... he was trying to make her feel better. "Hey, I really study this stuff. I don't mean like some people—I don't just do a five-minute Google search and figure I know all there is to know. I mean, I've read books, tons and tons of them. I could quote you stuff all day about the Ancient Egyptians!"

Danny peered down at her sketch. "Wow! Wonderful sketch, Isabel."

Isabel started to cough. "Danny, this isn't even a sketch. This is lines!"

"Ah-HAH! *Methinks the lady doth protest too much*! That was a Shakespearean quote, by the way. You like Shakespeare, *si*?"

"What?" Isabel asked, "Danny ..." She was almost in tears. "I just want to draw. I don't speak Shakespeare." She searched for a glimmer of recognition in his eyes that he was beyond annoying and had turned into a major cling-on!

"Danny ... I gotta go ... now." Isabel tried to look like she had another destination in mind and turned to walk away as fast as she could.

Danny stopped and blinked. "What?" he asked. "Go where? *Adónde va usted*?"

"See ya!" She waved over her shoulder as she hurried off to another room where on the way in she had spied a funny painting of a boy wearing a dress. It was an American painting from the 17th century called "Robert Gibbs at 4½ Years." Isabel thought the little boy with long hair looked funny in his long gown, but she supposed that was the style back in early America. As Isabel settled down to work, she took a deep breath and tried to remember that drawing was what she did to relax.

She jotted down a few figures and started to get lost in her sketch. This is nice, she thought. Suddenly, she heard footsteps behind her. Then she heard it. "*Señorita Isabel ...*"

Isabel jumped up and hurried away. With each step she took she could hear Danny's untied sneakers clomp-clomping behind her. They were getting closer and closer.

It was like Marty trailing around after Avery! Only Marty was sweet and loveable, and Danny was like a sticky, gooey piece of gum you couldn't get off your clothes, no matter how hard you tried.

Thank goodness Maeve and Katani are in New York, she thought as she raced through the halls looking for Avery and Charlotte. The only thing making her happy right now was that at least her friends were having a good time. Clearly *she* wasn't having fun. Not at all! Danny Pellegrino was slowly but surely leeching all the fun out of her trip.

PART TWO

WORTH THE TRIP

CHAPTER 11

❧

CLASHING STYLES

IT WAS ONLY 9:30 on Friday, and Katani was already frantic

Michelle had to be at the *Teen Beat* fashion show venue super early, and Katani wanted to go with her to experience as much of the show as possible. Katani set her alarm clock for 7:00 a.m. sharp and was up, showered, and dressed by 7:15 a.m. She put on a little lip gloss so the fashion show people could see she was well groomed but still professional.

At 7:30, Katani sat down with Michelle to eat breakfast: a glass of orange juice and Michelle's delicious scrambled eggs with cheddar cheese, onion, and bacon. Michelle asked her if she was excited and Katani nodded, "Oh Michelle, this is a dream come true!"

Michelle gulped down her orange juice and said, "My first fashion show was the sweetest thing ever. You'll want to make sure you are on time so you don't miss anything."

Katani was all set to go. Maeve, on the other hand, was not. She was still out cold on the pullout couch. The long "Zzzz …" sounds coming from the study indicated that she had no intention of waking up any time soon.

It was a little after 8:00 when Michelle glanced at her watch and reluctantly said, "K, I really have to go now."

"Of course," Katani assured her. She wanted to be mature, though her heart was sinking. "I understand. We'll be right behind you."

"I know you will," Michelle said, though there was doubt upon her face. She dug into a striped leather handbag and handed Katani some cash. "Here. This is cab fare to the Teen Beat office. The fashion show is being held on the 29th floor in the grand ballroom. I'll write down the address for you. It's not far from here at all. You think you can find it?"

"Oh, sure," Katani said, trying to sound confident. "How hard can it be?"

Michelle carefully scribbled down the office address, her office phone number, and her cell phone number. "The front door locks automatically, so just pull it closed when you leave. Andrew's the doorman who's on duty during the day at my building. He's really nice. Ask him to get you a cab and then just tell the driver the address. Cab drivers know where everything is in this city. And don't worry if it's too busy for a cab—you can always take the subway."

"The subway?" Katani asked doubtfully.

"Well of course, silly. Everyone takes the subway in New York. It's much cheaper than a taxi and just as quick and easy. Besides, the stop is only a few blocks away. Andrew will tell you how to get there." Michelle glanced at her watch. "Yikes! OK now I *really* have to run. I'll see you soon, Katani!"

She gave Katani a hug and was off in a flash. People in New York seemed to move a lot faster than they did in Brookline!

The moment the door slammed shut behind Michelle, Katani heard a loud thump followed by a yawn coming from the study down the hall. The door burst open and out stumbled Maeve, her eyes still half closed. "Sleeping Beauty is awake!" Maeve announced, stretching groggily. "And has to shower like *WHOA!*"

Katani watched as Maeve tramped down to the bathroom. The shower seemed to go on forever. When the water finally shut off, Katani heard the sound of Maeve's voice belting out a song from an old Broadway show: "*Come on along and listen to … the lullaby of Broadway!*"

Katani summoned up all the patience she could muster. The sooner Maeve ate, the sooner they could get their show on the road. Katani quickly laid out breakfast for Maeve and called her to come in and eat. Ten minutes later, Maeve appeared in the kitchen. Her face was scrubbed, but her hair was soaking wet.

"Oh, Katani, you didn't have to do that! Thanks!" Maeve exclaimed when she saw the eggs and toast on a plate. She slid into a chair and began to drink her orange juice as though she had not a worry in the world.

Katani could feel her face getting warm. This was the day she had been looking forward to for weeks. In fact, she had been waiting for this day her whole life. She couldn't wait to be a part of the big fashion show, and she was already running late.

"I think," Katani suggested as politely as she could manage, "that we'd better get going now. Michelle is already there, and she expects us to come very soon. She even gave me cab fare."

"Oh. OK." Maeve cast a longing glance at the pitcher of orange juice but obediently got up. "I'll be just a minute," she promised.

That minute turned into fifty …

Maeve simply could not make up her mind on what to wear. She had brought enough with her for a month, Katani thought, and she had to try on each outfit and scrutinize her appearance in the mirror before deciding that no, this wasn't right at all. These pants made her look like a kid, and that sweatshirt was too garish, and these jeans were too informal for an office, and … Katani lost track of the reasons Maeve gave for each change of outfit.

Katani was so upset she was ready to cry. She wanted so badly to come across as professional on her big fashion debut. Professionals were always on time. Professionals made do with whatever they had. Professionals got the job done. And arriving more than an hour after everyone else didn't make her a look like a professional—it made her look like a kid who couldn't keep up!

She bit her lip. Why didn't Maeve understand how important this was to her? She was about to pound on the door when Maeve finally popped out of the room.

"I think I've got it," Maeve finally announced brightly. She came out of the study wearing jeans, a crisp, white shirt, and a light pink cable-knit sweater. She rolled the cuffs of the shirt over the sweater and was sporting what she called "the popped collar."

Katani stared at her. "That was the first outfit you put on!"

"I know. I guess it's like Dorothy's lesson in *The Wizard of Oz*. I had to try everything else to know that I had it right the first time!" Maeve flashed Katani a friendly smile. "Anyway, I'm ready now. I won't even waste time doing my hair again." She showed off her freshly washed red hair that she'd spent at least a half hour drying and styling. "See? Just these two little barrettes. Very simple. I don't want to hold you up. Come on, let's hurry."

Katani wondered if Maeve knew the meaning of the word hurry. "Oh, I'm hurrying," Katani said sarcastically.

"Now, do I have everything?" Maeve looked around doubtfully for a minute. She swung her pink jacket over her shoulder, but a worried look still plagued her face.

"I'm sure you're all set," Katani said dismissively. She had waited for Maeve long enough, and now she was done. She turned and marched out the door with Maeve scuttling behind her.

Once they got out of the apartment, Katani assumed it would be relatively easy to ride the elevator down to the lobby and catch a cab. But she hadn't accounted for Maeve's enormous pocketbook. It was a retro carpet bag that was about size of a small child. Maeve loved it—and started complaining about it as soon as they got into the elevator.

"This is soooo heavy," Maeve groaned.

"Then leave it in the apartment!" Katani snapped. She could feel her patience slipping away and feared it was coming across in her voice.

Maeve looked hurt. "I can't! I've got all kinds of important stuff in here. Besides, if I go back, it'll make us late."

Late? Katani wanted to yell at her. We were late half an hour ago—now we might as well be Rip Van Winkle!

But she bit her lip. When the elevator doors jerkily slid open on the ground floor Katani was through them in the wink of an eye. Maeve followed, shifting the heavy bag from one shoulder to the other for comfort.

Katani spotted a man in a dark red uniform standing outside as soon as she came through the doors. "Excuse me, are you Andrew?" she asked.

He smiled. "You must be Michelle's cousin," he said. And as Maeve huffed and puffed out the door behind her, he added,

"And friend."

"That's right," Katani agreed, grinning back at him. She began to feel more cheerful now that she had this jolly doorman looking after her. Outside it was sunny and bright, which further lifted her spirits. "Michelle said you could help us get a cab?"

Andrew looked as if she had just asked the unthinkable. "Now? Oh, honey, you won't get a cab now. You can't catch a cab in this neighborhood until rush hour is over. I recommend you walk up two blocks to the subway."

Maeve looked utterly beside herself at the idea of lugging her barge of a bag up and down subway station stairs. "Is that really the only option?" she asked dejectedly. "There has to be another way ..."

"I'm afraid not," Andrew said sympathetically. "But cheer up, little lady. It's real easy." He pointed in the right direction. "See over there? That's the station. You catch the number one train, the Seventh Avenue local. It stops in Times Square." Katani listened carefully while Maeve scanned the street, unwilling to give up the idea that an empty cab might pass by.

"I've got it," Katani said finally. "Thanks, Andrew," she called over her shoulder as they walked away.

"Are you *sure* we can't take a cab?"

"You heard Andrew. It's too late. There were cabs here an hour ago, but now we have to take the subway."

"But subways can be dangerous!" Maeve turned pale.

Katani rolled her eyes, exasperated. "Come on, Maeve, even Michelle said that we might have to take the subway, and she told me it was fine. It'll be full of people, and it's broad daylight. Lots of kids our age take the subway every single day, and they don't have a problem."

"But what if we get lost?" Maeve looked genuinely

nervous at the thought.

"We won't. I have a great sense of direction." Katani was now getting seriously annoyed. She felt like she was the only one who cared about being grown up and responsible! But then she caught a glimpse of Maeve's big, scared eyes, and she remembered this was her very good friend who'd gone to bat for her and made sure she could even be there right now. "Wait!" Katani said. She took the piece of paper that had the *Teen Beat* address on it. She doubled checked once more and then shoved it into Maeve's pocket. "Now you have the address too, so no matter what happens we'll be just fine."

"OK," Maeve said, sounding a little more cheerful. "If you really think it'll be all right." They made their way up the streets to the subway. Katani led the way swinging a tiny black purse of her own design, while Maeve lagged behind, struggling to keep the heavy tapestry bag on her shoulder. What exactly did she have in there? Katani wondered.

They caught the uptown train at the Sheridan Square station. Katani felt a definite sense of accomplishment that they were at last headed in the right direction and with some speed! It was extremely crowded on the train, and there were no vacant seats when they boarded. So they stood, holding on as best they could, with Maeve still shifting the bag every few minutes.

"Ow, this thing hurts," she complained once the train started moving. Katani said nothing. She knew if she opened her mouth she'd probably point out the foolishness of bringing a bag that size in the first place.

When Katani didn't respond, Maeve persisted. "Did you notice the view from Michelle's study? When I looked out this morning, it was so beautiful. It looks right over the square, you know? Did you see that last night, or was it too dark to see?"

"I don't know," Katani said briefly. "I wasn't paying attention." All she wanted to think about was working with Michelle on the fashion show. She'd had enough of Maeve's jabbering yesterday in the car, and it looked like Maeve was determined to do more of the same today. Katani didn't know if she would be able to stand it.

"Hey, check out the artists," Maeve said, nodding to a pair of tall guys in colorful ponchos and weird hats. They looked like the kind you saw in old photos of Western cowboys. "They must be painters, don't you think, or photographers? Their outfits are so wild! I love it!"

Katani didn't reply. At the next stop, a group of young men and women came on, most wearing backpacks and sporting NYU sweatshirts. "College students," Maeve whispered.

Would she ever stop? Katani wondered. Did Maeve have to comment on everything? It didn't occur to Katani that Maeve was talking more than usual, partly because Katani was so quiet.

"Oh, look at the cute baby!" Maeve cooed, nudging Katani and pointing at a young woman seated several rows back. They could see the baby, folded into a soft blanket in the woman's lap, its face peaceful in sleep, its little fists clenched.

Katani's face softened. The baby was cute. And Maeve did notice an awful lot about people. She could see little slices of life and wonderful details that Katani herself would never stop to observe. *Maybe,* she thought a little guiltily, *she sees how impatient I am right now to get to* Teen Beat *and she's just trying to make me feel better—in her own Maeve-ish way.*

"Isn't it cute?" Maeve asked again.

"Whoa—this is our stop!" Katani said, catching a glimpse of the Times Square station sign. "Come on!"

They poured out onto the platform along with at least

❁

thirty other people. "This way," Katani said, after glancing left and right. She led the way toward the exit stairs, weaving neatly in and out of the various groups of pedestrians in front of her. After so long, Katani couldn't believe that she was finally so close to her destination. She could hardly wait!

"Ouch, hang on. This bag is killing me! I think there's a pin sticking out or something," Maeve called once she was safely on the platform and clear of the train. She heaved a sigh of relief as she placed it on the ground. Maeve felt silly. Earlier, she'd thought that a brush, some makeup, a mirror, and pictures of famous models and actors who could be at the show were all really important things to have with her at all times in New York. Now she realized that Charlotte had been absolutely right. Traveling light was essential, especially when she was on her feet so much.

Charlotte wouldn't have approved of her footwear, either, Maeve thought, awkwardly looking down at her flashy pink boots. She'd packed the comfortable shoes Charlotte picked out but left them at Michelle's. She thought she would be so embarrassed in front of these well-dressed New Yorkers if she was caught wearing sneakers all over town! Unfortunately, her feet were already starting to ache. And every well-dressed New Yorker who passed was wearing comfortable shoes.

She managed to swing her bag onto her shoulder in a momentarily comfortable position. "OK, let's go!" she said, but when she looked up, Katani was far ahead of her.

"Hey, Kgirl! Wait up!"

Katani did not turn around, and the crowds seemed to get thicker and thicker as Maeve got closer to the stairs. She made a beeline for the staircase in the center, where she had seen Katani go. She clung to the sturdy metal railing as she tottered up the stone steps in her high-heeled boots. The bag was miraculously in the right position for once, and she found the pin that was sticking in to her shoulder and closed it. But now she could feel the blisters on her feet growing with each step. *Tonight,* she promised herself grimly, *I'll put away these dumb boots and wear my sneakers for the rest of the weekend!*

As she approached the top of the steps, Maeve saw the young woman from the train carrying the baby she'd noticed. It looked so sweet, with its head lying on its mother's shoulder, its little fists still clenched, looking completely relaxed and trusting. Maeve smiled as the young woman went swiftly past her.

And then as she looked to the top of the stairs again, she thought her heart would stop.

Katani was no longer in sight.

She'd been right there a second ago! Right at the top of the stairs—Maeve had been watching! Suddenly, there was no sign of her!

Panicked, Maeve pounded up the last few steps and emerged into the heart of Times Square. There had to be a million people around her. Her chance of finding Katani was about as good as finding a needle in a haystack.

Maeve looked around in horror. Everyone in New York moved so *fast!* They all seemed to know exactly where they were going and wasted no time in getting there. Maeve had never seen anyone, other than Olympic athletes, move faster! She was completely overwhelmed.

She looked in all directions as quickly as she could. It was almost impossible to spot any one person because the crowds were so dense. And she felt paralyzed. *This is like one of those nightmares where you want to move but can't,* she thought to herself. With her heavy bag and pinching boots Maeve slowly tromped on, craning her neck for any sign of Katani.

Then it dawned on her: she was actually in Times Square. For years she had imagined standing in the middle of Times Square as a famous actress, waving graciously to crowds, completely confident in the spotlight, relishing the long theatrical history of Broadway ... The Great White Way.

Now she was not so confident. Across the street there was a man with a boa constrictor writhing around his body. Next to him a lady wearing a cardboard sign was trying to talk to anyone who passed by. "Toto, it looks like we're not in Kansas anymore," Maeve said to herself. What would she do if she couldn't find Katani? With no directions, Maeve didn't think she could find the *Teen Beat* offices if her life depended on it. She was ready to burst into tears.

Then a glint of gold caught her eye. It was Katani's hand-painted golden scarf. And above the scarf, thank goodness, was the back of Katani's head. Katani was just stepping onto a curb across the street.

Oh, what a relief! Maeve didn't even feel her feet aching or the strap of her bag cutting into her shoulder. She ran frantically across the street keeping her eyes glued to Katani. "BEEEP!" Suddenly Maeve heard the screech of tires and the shriek of car horns. She looked to her left. Yellow cabs all around were jerking to a halt, and the drivers were leaning out the windows, their faces snarling. At her.

"What the heck are you doing?" shouted one guy. "Are ya tryin' to cause an accident ... or get yerself killed?!"

Maeve, horrified, just gaped at him. She couldn't think what to say.

"Hey, doofus! Get outta the street already!" shouted another angry cab driver.

A third was rolling down the driver's-side window. Maeve noticed that this one was a tough-looking woman, but she hoped the woman understood how terrified she was. Maybe she'd even stick up for her and tell those guys to stop mouthing off.

Not exactly. The woman rolled down the window and shouted, "Move it or lose it, kid, I ain't got all day!"

Maeve's heart, which had been pounding hard before, now felt like it was going to explode. She thought she was going to collapse right in the middle of Times Square. Maeve took a deep breath and called "Sorry. I'm sorry!" to the cabbies as she ran across the street.

She was furious at Katani and wondered what she would say when she reached her. *How could she have left me alone like that*? Maeve asked herself.

She followed Katani's distinctive duffle coat up one more block and then finally caught up. Maeve grabbed her shoulder and cried, "Hey! Why did you ditch me, Katani?"

"Excuse me?" The girl in the duffle coat turned around. "Do I know you?" She was at least ten years older than Maeve and Katani.

The puzzled girl stared at Maeve, who shrank back, frightened. She didn't know what New Yorkers did to strange young girls who yanked them by the shoulder—even if it was an honest mistake.

"I'm so sorry," Maeve mumbled. "I thought you were my friend."

The girl nodded and her face stopped looking so grim. "You lost?"

"Yes," Maeve choked back.

"You need help?" the girl asked.

Maeve wasn't sure how her father would feel about her getting help from a stranger. She shook her head and walked away, leaving the girl looking confused behind her. Maeve thought she really would die right there. How could she find this place if she couldn't ask strangers for help? This was a terrible, terrible moment. Maeve felt her eyes begin to fill up.

She knew that in an instant the dab of mascara she had put on would be in two long streaks down her face. Maeve reached in her pocket to grab a tissue and something incredible happened. There was no tissue! The only thing in her pocket was the slip of paper Katani had given her with *Teen Beat*'s office address and phone number written on it. Hallelujah! This would save her. Now at least she knew where she was supposed to go.

Then Maeve remembered that her father had given her his cell phone last night. She could call her mom and ask her to look up directions on the Internet. That would help. It couldn't be far, since Katani had made them get off the subway in Times Square. *It's probably not more than a block or two away*, Maeve told herself. Like Michelle's apartment last night. *Everything in New York is sort of compressed. I'll just call Mom and find out. Maybe Katani's even there by now.*

She opened her enormous tapestry bag to get the phone and then froze. She knew she forgot something in the apartment that morning, but Katani had rushed her out so quickly! The cell phone was still on the charger in the study, exactly where she'd left it last night. *Big* help.

CHAPTER 12

ᚹ

THE ARTFUL DODGER

"HEY, IZZY HAS BEEN GONE A WHILE," Avery noticed, looking around the Mummy Room. She'd gotten so absorbed in the sarcophaguses and mummies and reading about the embalming process that she'd completely forgotten about Isabel and her mummy-phobia.

"Where *did* she go?" Charlotte looked around, puzzled. "I could have sworn she was right back there sketching."

"Me too." Avery inspected the gallery. "Hey, Char, check it out!" Behind a large column, at the other end of the room, stuck out a snippet of a red shirt. They crept over to find Isabel hunched over her sketchpad, looking like she wished she could disappear.

Charlotte and Avery looked at each other. "What is she doing?" Avery asked. "Hey, Izzy! Rejoin the living, will you?"

Isabel, startled, quickly put a finger on her lips to shush Avery, but it was too late. Danny's head spun around at the mention of Isabel's name. Isabel knew it was only a matter of time before he'd corner her with more mind-numbing Egyptian trivia, speckled with Spanish phrases. Maybe he really liked her, or maybe he just wanted to be her friend, but one more minute with Danny and she was sure she would scream. Crouched behind the column, she tilted her head to warn Charlotte and Avery of Danny's impending approach.

"Uh-oh," Avery said, turning around. "Trouble."

Charlotte saw it too.

Isabel motioned for the girls to lean in closer and whispered, "It's been like this all day!" Isabel looked like she didn't know if she was going to burst out laughing or crying. She whispered a little louder. "Danny won't leave me alone. It's like he can't wait to tell me everything he knows about everything." Isabel beckoned them to circle in front of her. "You can be my shield."

Avery glanced at Charlotte and grinned. "Looks like it's time for Operation BSG Rescue," she whispered. "Follow me!"

Avery did a 180-degree jump and landed directly between Isabel and Danny. "Oh, hi, Danny," she said, trying to sound casual. "How are you liking the museum?"

Danny looked flustered as he tried to catch a glimpse over Avery's shoulder. "Umm, it's good ..." he stuttered.

In a minute, Charlotte was crowding in next to Avery so Danny was completely blocked off from his favorite person in the world. Isabel gave her friends her most grateful smile.

"OK, well, have a nice day!" Avery told him, then exclaimed, "Hey, Isabel! What a surprise!" She grabbed Isabel's arm. "I've been looking all over for you! I really, really need to um, go to the ladies' room, don't you?"

"Oh, totally!" Isabel managed. "*Excellent* idea!" She stuffed her sketchbook in her bag. Before Danny was able to say more than, "Hey Isabel, did you know that ...?" the girls were off. In a minute, they had made it to the ladies' room at the end of the hall and piled in.

"This isn't far enough," Isabel said. "I bet you anything he'll come after me!" She opened the door of the ladies' room a crack and moaned. "Oh, no. He's already there waiting for us!"

The other girls looked out too. Sure enough, Danny was sauntering down the hall at a casual but deliberate pace about a hundred yards away. He pretended to be looking at the pictures but the girls could see him stealing glances at the ladies' room door.

"He'd make an excellent body guard!" Avery giggled.

"I think we should keep going," Isabel said in a low voice. "Past those glass cabinets. Quick!" The girls slinked out of the bathroom one by one, and—pressed to the wall *Mission Impossible* style—shuffled past some old-looking glass cabinets called "vitrines."

"There!" Charlotte pointed. They rounded the corner and found themselves in a nice long hallway with doors on either side. Isabel breathed a sigh of relief. It was soothingly quiet in the empty hallway.

Charlotte peered out around the corner. "Hey guys, I think we lost him. He must think we're still in the ladies' room."

Isabel leaned gratefully against one of the tall columns, tilting her head back to look up at the high ceiling. "You guys saved my life," she said. "He's been following me all day long."

"And doing what?" Charlotte asked.

Isabel groaned. "Telling me absolutely everything he knows about Ancient Egypt. I mean, some of it was interesting, but he just wouldn't stop. It's like he drank ten cups of coffee or something. Oh! And get this! He keeps randomly using Spanish words that don't always make sense, like what a '*bonita* idea'!" Isabel complained. "And he says my name with a Spanish accent."

Charlotte covered her mouth to keep from laughing. "Oh

geesh!" Avery said, rolling her eyes.

"Tell me about it!" Isabel agreed. "He was completely in my way when I was trying to sketch. There are so many cool things to draw here, and I haven't been able to finish even one!" She threw down her bag, totally exasperated.

"Well, did you tell him to bug off?" Avery asked.

Isabel sighed. "I would have, but I was afraid I might hurt his feelings. I'd hate to do that. I tried to give him hints, but boy, he just doesn't get it! And to think, I was looking forward to this trip so much."

"So wait, he really spoke Spanish?" Charlotte asked.

Isabel closed her eyes and shook her head. "Oh you should have heard him. There are American ducks who speak better Spanish than him."

Avery started to giggle, and soon Charlotte and Isabel joined in. The thought of Danny trying to impress Isabel by speaking bad Spanish to her was hilarious. Soon Isabel felt herself slowly regaining her usual upbeat attitude ... now that her friends were nearby and Danny wasn't.

"We probably shouldn't stay here for too much longer," Charlotte said when they'd finally stopped laughing. "We need to get back to our group."

Avery flattened herself against the wall and peeked cautiously around the corner. "Uh-oh," she reported. "Danny's pretending to look at the dioramas with scenes of the Nile and pyramids."

"And he'll keep looking at them until Isabel shows up again," Charlotte said grimly. "Well, we can't stay here forever. And what about our teachers? Ms. R and Ms. Weston will be worried about us."

Avery cracked up again. "I'll bet Ms. Rodriguez won't even notice we're gone ... she's probably too busy trying to find Ms. Weston!" The other two girls burst into laughter again. Poor Ms. Weston was never going to live down her reputation for being "lost in space."

Avery peeked around the corner again, but this time her eyes widened. "OK, bad news! Danny's left the diorama and he's coming down the hall, right toward us! Abort mission!"

"We need to get out of here," Isabel said nervously.

Avery looked down the long corridor. "Hey, there's an open door," she said. "Come on, let's hide in there!"

Before the other girls could protest, she'd seized each one by the arm and hurried them into the dim room. Avery quickly pulled the door in behind them, leaving it open a crack.

"Whoa!" Charlotte said in a delighted voice, when her eyes adjusted to the low light.

Isabel looked around and her face erupted into a smile. There must have been some kind of storage room, because it was big, but crammed full of neat Egyptian objects. In the center of the room was a long wooden table, and on top of it were parts of various mummy cases and a number of small items with paper tags on them—hand mirrors, gold-plated combs, and tiny spoons. There were also charms made of glass and others of semi-precious stones. Earlier that day, the docent had told them that the charms were called amulets.

"Look at all this!" Isabel exclaimed. "These must be new additions to the collection or maybe things that need to be repaired. This is better than being in the main rooms! I'll bet no one except the museum personnel ever gets to see this. Oh, I've got to sketch *that*!"

"What?" Charlotte asked.

Isabel pointed at a funny-looking charm in the shape of a bug. "It's perfect. It's so tiny and unique. I think they call it a *scarab*. Danny told me the Egyptians were very fond of scarab jewelry."

"See Izzy, Danny did have some useful information," said a grinning Charlotte.

"Let's invite him in," joked Avery.

"Don't you dare," warned Isabel. "This'll just take a minute and then I'll have something to submit to *The Sentinel*." She leaned her sketchbook against the edge of the table and turned the charm just so to capture the light. Isabel quickly flipped to a blank page and began drawing.

"Um, Izzy, I don't want to make you nervous, but ..." Charlotte slowly tilted her head in the direction of a large mummy case resting against the wall.

Isabel's eyes widened. "I really don't think we should be in here," she said. "Come on, let's just go."

"OK, don't panic," Charlotte said as she inspected the mummy. "It's sealed shut! We have nothing to worry about."

"Besides, Danny's still out there," Avery reminded her. "Wouldn't leaving kind of defeat the purpose?" Avery had made one circle around the storage room and now was on her knees by the door peering through the keyhole. "Don't worry. Danny will get bored in no time. There's barely any art in this hallway! I'm sure he'll leave soon."

She pulled over a straight wooden chair and sat down next to the keyhole. "I'll be on Danny patrol. Go ahead and draw, Iz, but make it quick. I'll let you know when the coast is clear."

So Isabel drew, Charlotte paced, and Avery stood guard. They definitely had NOT planned on spending their field trip hidden in a dim, dusty storage room! The real question was, when would Danny disappear?

Isabel M.

CHAPTER 13

ભ

A SCARE IN TIMES SQUARE

EVEN THOUGH SHE HAD BEEN to New York before with her parents, today Maeve stood in the middle of Times Square feeling like a clueless tourist. She couldn't get used to all the people bustling around her. No one looked at anyone else as they rushed around, and she was sure that they'd crash into each other at any moment. Everyone, it seemed, was somehow comfortable on this frenzied city street—everyone except her.

Maeve felt totally out of place, from her attitude to her outfit. Half of the people she saw wore stark black dresses or suits, and the other half were in casual jeans. These were the clothes she'd rejected as either too old-fashioned or not special enough for New York!

Maeve prided herself on her edgy fashion sense, and the feeling that it had just deserted her—along with Katani and everything else—right in the middle of the world's most fashionable city, was almost too much for her.

OK, Maeve, get a grip, she told herself. *At least I have the address of the* Teen Beat *offices. There HAS to be someone around here who can tell me how to get there!*

She looked around doubtfully. At mid-morning, finding someone she could trust to direct her to the magazine's offices looked like a tough job. She could hear her mother's voice in her head cautioning, "Maeve, whatever you do, do *not* to talk to strangers!"

She clutched her big bag closer to her. It had become so heavy that it felt like a bar of iron on her shoulder, but she wouldn't be able to stand it if someone grabbed it away! It was the last thing she had that made her feel even slightly normal. Why had she insisted on wearing a pink jacket, of all things, and pink boots, which were killing her feet? Was she sticking out like a sore pink thumb? People were probably thinking to themselves, *Yikes*! That girl *must* be from out of town!

Stay cool, stay focused, Maeve reminded herself. The problem was she couldn't—she was too nervous. A thousand thoughts were buzzing through her head: *Should I find a phone? Should I ask someone on the street for directions? Should I call my dad? Should I call* Teen Beat? *Should I find a policeman? Should I do all of the above?*

Finally, after taking a few deep breaths, she decided to find a store and ask the people who worked there to help her out with directions. It was a public setting, and plus, the people who worked right in Times Square would surely know their way around. Maeve ducked into a store that sold candy, newspapers, and hot drinks and immediately headed for the counter.

The woman behind the register was surrounded by customers. Her hands moved like lightning. She'd take a bill and press a button, and then a bell would ring, and in a moment the woman's hand would reach out with the perfect change. With a nod, she would turn over the money and receipt, all in one blurred movement. Maeve tried to wait for a lull, but she was quickly learning that there was no lull in New York City.

After waiting patiently for a minute, she finally got her chance, "I'm lost. Could you please tell me how to get here?" She slid the paper with *Teen Beat*'s address across the counter in front of the woman.

The woman quickly blinked at the paper. "Oh, yeah. That's a block over and one block down from here. Walk down a block, turn left at the corner and then it's on your left."

"What?" Maeve desperately tried to understand the clerk's directions, but her rapid-fire delivery made that impossible. "Could you please repeat that just one more time?"

The woman looked aggravated. As she opened her mouth, at least a dozen people approached the counter at once, snatching up papers, asking for coffee, and holding their money out so they'd be served next.

Maeve knew she couldn't compete with the store's hurried customers. Not only did they know exactly where they were going, but they actually had money for the cashier. She went back to her business and Maeve was back to being LOST. What was she going to do now?

Maeve was considering getting a cab to take her directly to *Teen Beat*, no matter what it cost, when she heard a male voice behind her say, "Pardon me, are you lost, young lady?"

Maeve whirled around. She was surprised to see that this helpful stranger was not only young and polite. He was … well, absolutely dreamy!

The man stood tall with a slim frame. His chestnut hair fell around his face at just the right semi-long length and matched a pair of deep, dark eyes and high cheekbones. He paid for a copy of *The New York Times*, and instead of pocketing the change, he dropped it all—bills included—into the tip jar.

Maeve was unaware that she hadn't responded until the dreamy man repeated, "Are you lost? Maybe we can help you." It was then that she noticed his soft British accent. Somehow his accent made him seem less like a stranger and more like a chummy friend you would invite over for tea, she thought. She looked at his face and felt like she had seen him before, but she couldn't put her finger on it. For the first time since Katani disappeared, Maeve began to feel a little safer. She even managed to smile.

He smiled back. Maeve felt her heart make a *ka-thump* in her chest.

"Thank you, sir," she said, feeling more confident. "I am a little lost. I'm looking for this address." She showed him the paper.

"Oh, what a coincidence!" piped up a female voice next to him. Maeve turned to see a slender young woman at his side. She too had a British accent. Her light blonde hair was stylishly cropped to her chin and her clothes were fabulously mod. Next to these people, Maeve began to feel a bit babyish in her ultra-pink ensemble. "We're headed to the very same place! Are you going to the *Teen Beat* fashion show too?" Maeve stared. She couldn't believe it. That was the last thing she expected to hear.

There was no way that this could be some kind of trick. How else could they *possibly* know about the fashion show? "I'm Bea, by the way," the woman said with a warm smile.

"Let's get out of this madhouse, shall we?" the man said kindly to Maeve. "It's getting awfully crowded in here, don't you think?"

Maeve hadn't noticed. To her, everything in New York

seemed crowded. As they made their way out of the stuffy little store, she noticed that everyone they passed stopped what they were doing to stare at her. No—not just at her, but at … well, at *all of them*! Why? she wondered. Maybe they were trying to figure out how two ultra-stylish people ever got mixed up with a girl wearing all pink and toting around a gigantic bag made out of a rug!

Oh well! thought Maeve. She was willing to chance looking out of place if these super cool Brits could point her in the right direction.

"Now look," said the man in his delightful accent. In the light of day, Maeve thought he looked even hunkier! "We're going to the exact same place as you. And it's not far at all. You can come with us if you like."

Maeve stood uncertainly. They did seem awfully friendly. Even though her instincts told her she could trust them, Maeve wished she had some sort of solid proof.

It was as though Bea could read her mind. "Hold on a moment! I have something in here about the show, I think." The woman opened up her tiny designer handbag and fumbled around inside. "Ah-ha! Here we go!" Triumphantly, Bea produced a lavishly printed invitation to the *Teen Beat* Magazine Fashion Show. Maeve had seen one just like it on Michelle's desk that morning. Apparently, they really were going to the fashion show.

"Well, what do you think?" the man asked with another smile. "The only thing that could get in the way between us and this show are these New York street signs. Even though they do number the streets so cleverly, I still get lost. I've always been a dreadful mess when it comes to math and numbers," he confessed. Bea laughed and Maeve also found herself smiling. Maeve thought she should practice a British accent—it sounded so delightfully delightful!

"All right," Maeve said cautiously. But she told herself she'd stay a few feet behind them, just in case.

Maeve soon became genuinely comfortable. Bea and her friend thoughtfully gave her plenty of space as she walked slightly behind them up the street. Truth or dare, Maeve thought that she should be ready to run in case they turned out to be kidnapping alien terrorists sent from the mother ship to bring a certain red-headed girl back to the planet Urg to teach everyone about hip hop dancing. But instead, the friendly couple would turn around every once in a while to give her an encouraging smile and tell her how bewildering they found New York.

"It's just awful to be a stranger in a new city," Bea commented. "I get so confused!"

"Totally!" Maeve agreed. She completely understood how they felt.

Bea stopped and pointed out a modern, glassy building. "But look! I do think we've actually made it!" She looked up at the building and checked the number against her invitation. "Yes, here we are."

Maeve felt a wave of relief. Was it possible that she, Maeve Kaplan-Taylor, had reached the right place? And she had done it, basically, as an independent girl. After a long and overwhelming morning, Maeve finally began to feel like her optimistic self again. *How wonderful to be in New York!* she thought as she gave her red mane a toss.

As they started toward the lobby doors, Maeve was convinced that everyone was turning to stare at them. What was going on? Did she really look so out of place that sophisticated New Yorkers would stop what they were doing and gape at her? Maeve remembered the man with the snake

✿

outside the subway station and thought, there *have* to be crazier looking people than me in this city!

But for sure, these people were staring at *something*.

CHAPTER 14

⊛

"HITCH YOUR WAGON TO A STAR"

~ RALPH WALDO EMERSON

BEFORE THEY TOOK THREE STEPS into the lobby, a security guard seated behind a large paneled desk stopped them. "Names, please?"

"Maeve Kaplan-Taylor," Maeve said hesitantly. "I'm not sure I'm in the right place."

"Oh, Ms. Kaplan-Taylor, they are waiting for you upstairs," he said with a look of concern. Maeve's stomach flip-flopped. She hoped she hadn't caused too much trouble by getting lost.

The security guard looked down a printed list on his desk. "You're here for the fashion show, correct?"

"Oh yes!" Maeve confirmed with a smile.

"All right, Ms. Kaplan-Taylor. Here's your badge," he said smoothly. "You're all set. It's on the 29th floor."

Maeve took the badge and thanked him. When her two companions stepped up behind her, something very strange happened. The security guard didn't ask them a thing. Instead, he smiled warmly and said, "Well now. Good morning. Welcome. Here are your VIP passes. When you get

⚘

to the 29th floor, someone will be there to assist you."

"Thank you," said the man. He took the badges and led Bea and Maeve to the elevators. Maeve was surprised that the British couple wasn't asked for their names, as she had been, but she supposed they'd been here before.

Maeve felt the stares again as she crossed the lobby. When they walked by, people stopped mid-sentence and pointed. How embarrassing! She was about to go into a real New York fashion show, and her fashion statement was a flop!

She hunched her shoulders together and tried to make herself invisible as they waited for the elevator.

Bea looked at her, puzzled. "Are you cold?" she asked.

"No … just embarrassed," Maeve admitted. "I guess I shouldn't have worn all this pink. All the people I see on the streets are wearing navy and black. People keep looking at me like I'm nuts!"

"Oh, no!" Bea said. "I think that outfit looks terrific on you! And I *love* your boots!"

"You do?" Maeve was astonished. "Really?"

"You look adorable. And that handbag is totally wicked!"

"Then why is everyone staring?" Maeve asked.

The elevator jangled to a stop and the doors opened. "Oh, I wouldn't worry about it," Bea said vaguely as they stepped on. "I'm sure it has nothing to do with what you're wearing."

Maeve glanced sideways at the gorgeous guy who hadn't spoken at all since he picked up the badges. He was smiling slightly, eyes fixed straight ahead, as though he knew a little secret. Maeve wished she could remember why he looked so familiar. Where had she seen that dreamy confidence before?

The elevator was much swifter than the clunky old one in Michelle's building. In under a minute, they were whisked up to the 29th floor. The doors slid smoothly open.

The first person Maeve saw was Katani.

Maeve noticed immediately that Katani was teary-eyed and frantically trying to zip up her coat. Next to her, Michelle was pulling on her own jacket, looking tense and frightened. Behind them were two policemen.

"Katani!" Maeve called, rushing out of the elevator. She hugged her friend in a fever of relief.

"Maeve! We were on our way out to look for you!" Katani cried. Suddenly Katani stopped hugging Maeve and looked at her accusingly. "Where have you been? What were you thinking, going off by yourself like that?"

Maeve gulped. "What do you mean? You left me behind in the subway." Now she was almost tearful, too. "You were in such a rush you never even noticed I was gone."

For a minute both girls just stood there, eyes welling with tears. Katani felt awful. Maeve was right. She had been so furious all morning that she had forgotten the most obvious thing: friends are the number-one priority. Being worried about Maeve was ten times worse than being worried about arriving at the fashion show late. And now that Maeve was here, she realized that she was happy—even happier than when she found out about this trip in the first place. "I'm sorry, Maeve."

Maeve hugged her. "No, it's OK. I'm just glad I found this place!"

When Michelle spotted the British couple standing quietly behind the girls, her eyes widened. "Oh, thank goodness ... Simon! You made it!"

Katani turned and gasped. She began to stare too. In fact, everyone in the hallway was staring. Some people were even pointing and whispering, but smiling the whole time.

Maeve turned to look at the man Michelle had called Simon, and her eyes widened. *Oh ... my ... gosh*!

Simon Blackstone! How could she not have known him? British heartthrob, star of the great new action movie *The Swashbuckler*, actor, rocker, and out-of-this-world hip hop dancer—and she, who knew his face from movies and magazines, hadn't even realized it!

I was rescued by Simon Blackstone, Maeve thought. *Is that too amazingly cool or what? This is the BEST day of my life!*

Michelle had already taken charge of the situation. She thanked the policemen for coming and apologized for having wasted their time.

"We're just glad everything turned out all right," they said very graciously. Maeve blushed as she thanked her rescuers and then began apologizing in over-the-top Maeve style for not recognizing them sooner. "I mean," she gushed to Simon, "you are one of my all-time favorite actors, if not my favorite. I like you even better than … You know, I am going to be an actress too someday … maybe you could …" Maeve noticed that Katani was frantically motioning for Maeve to "chill."

"Oh," she looked up at Simon, the biggest heartthrob on the planet. "I … I'm sorry … you must want to …" Simon flashed Maeve his famous, sparkling, devilish smile, the smile that made millions of girls all over the world scream "SIMON ROCKS!" Speechless, Maeve just bobbed her head at his gleaming white teeth. And then the unimaginable happened. Simon Blackstone, favorite movie star of Maeve Kaplan-Taylor, reached over and lifted Maeve's hand to his lips, brushed it lightly with a kiss and in his impossibly cool British accent said "Anytime, Luv."

Maeve grabbed Katani's hand and watched as Michelle led Simon and Bea to the magazine's conference room, where there was a brunch specially prepared just for them. Michelle turned to Katani and Maeve, noticing their overwhelmed expressions.

"Why don't you two freshen up?" she suggested. "I'll meet you right back in this conference room when you're done."

"You know that I can never wash this hand ... I mean, NEVER wash this hand ever again in my whole entire life. Someone should take a picture of this hand and put it in the Fan Hall of Fame," Maeve said as she walked to the ladies' room with Katani.

"OK. Maeve, explain this to me," Katani said the minute the girls were alone in the ladies' room. She was bursting with curiosity. "So you get totally lost in Times Square, in the middle of New York City. Then you come strolling in here with—who? Oh, right. *Simon Blackstone*! Maeve Kaplan-Taylor, how did you manage this? Speak now or I will be forced to make you speak," Katani said, laughing. "It just isn't possible that someone from Abigail Adams Junior High gets their hand kissed by Simon Blackstone. How on earth did you do it?"

"Oh, we didn't *just* come up in the same elevator," Maeve said, giggling a little in sheer relief. "He *found* me in Times Square—and brought me over here because he was worried about me."

"No!" Katani looked stunned. "That's incredible! He found you and *rescued* you?"

"Well—I guess he and Bea both did," Maeve said. She felt both giddy and calm, now that she was finally with Katani again. "He, of course, just sort of swept me up and carried me away." When she saw the doubtful look on Katani's face, she amended, "Well, not exactly. But I couldn't find the building and he and Bea said they were coming here anyway, so they asked me if I wanted to come along. And want to hear the craziest part? I was so panicked all morning it didn't occur to me who he was. Me! Can you imagine?! I didn't even really care who he was, as long as I found you." She looked over at Katani and gave her a warm smile.

"I was so scared when I couldn't find you!" Katani said. "I didn't go straight to Michelle's office. As soon as I got out of the subway and realized that you were missing, I waited and waited, and then I walked around in circles, thinking I'd find you behind me. Then after a while I thought maybe you had found your way here, so I rushed over. I told Michelle as soon as I saw her, and she called the police. When you got here we were just on our way out to look for you." She shook her head. "It was horrible!" And then the normally reserved Katani threw her arms around Maeve and gave her an unexpected Kgirl super hug.

"It's over now," Maeve said, hugging her friend and thinking back on how people had stared at her in the lobby and on the street. She turned to Katani and giggled. "You know, when people stared at us on the way here, I kept thinking it was because my outfit was all wrong. But Bea said she loved what I was wearing *and* she thought my bag was great! Gosh! I had absolutely no idea that everyone was staring at *him*." She shook her head and her cheeks turned as pink as her outfit. She'd been so sure there was something wrong with *her* that it never occurred to her that there was another, simpler explanation for why New Yorkers would stop and stare!

Katani stared at her now, too. "What?" Maeve said.

Katani shrugged and smiled. "Nothing," she said finally. "You do look cute. There's just one thing …" She handed Maeve a comb. "Here. Just a few strokes and you'll be all set!"

Maeve thanked her and began to rearrange her long, red tresses while Katani watched her in silence and a little wonder. She was just beginning to see what Bea, whom Michelle said was Simon's manager (*sigh*!), was talking about. That morning

Katani had looked at Maeve like she didn't have a clue about what to wear in New York City. When she decided to bring that retro bag, Katani began to get Mary Poppins flashbacks. But now she saw that Maeve's unique sense of style was pretty cool. She was drenched in pink, and what person—according to Ms. Razzberry Pink, proprietor of Maeve's favorite store, Think Pink—didn't feel good when they were covered in pink? Maybe Bea really did admire Maeve's daring ensemble.

Katani had always thought that her sense of style was the best because she followed what was going on in the world of fashion. But now she saw that her fashion sense was simply not the only way. Maybe she needed to expand her appreciation of fashion. Even if something wasn't really her taste, it didn't mean it wasn't perfect for someone else. How would she ever make it to the top of the fashion world if there were so many more things to learn? *Was it always going to be like this*? she wondered. Wouldn't she ever get to a point in life when she was finished learning?

"Girls!" Michelle rushed into the ladies' room just as Maeve combed her last strands of hair into place. "You won't believe who's here!"

Maeve put her hands on her hips, "Michelle, I get it! Simon Blackstone."

Michelle shook her head. "No! I mean, besides him!"

"Who?" Katani asked.

"A reporter from the local New York cable station, New York 1! They broadcast all over the five boroughs!"

Surprised, Katani looked at her cousin. Michelle was a member of the press herself. She dealt with the media every day. Why was this such a big deal?

Michelle didn't give her time to guess. "Wait! You haven't heard the best part! They found out there are two girls here from Boston who are interested in fashion careers, and they'd like to interview you both *right now*!"

"Wow!" Maeve shrieked, her blue eyes shining. "I'm going to be on camera?!"

"Exactly!" said Michelle.

"That's awesome! Hold on, I'm going to call Charlotte and tell her to turn on the TV!"

Katani stared at her. "They won't be able to see it, silly. It's only going to be on local news. And besides, they're still on the field trip."

"Ohh …" Maeve was clearly disappointed.

"Come on," Michelle said. "It'll be fun. They're looking to do the interviews right now, before we get started with the show. So you'd better hustle!"

Maeve was bubbling over with excitement as Michelle led them down the hall. Katani, however, was quiet. Since when had Maeve been interested in a career in *fashion*?

CHAPTER 15

℞

WALK THE WALK,
TALK THE TALK

WHEN THEY STEPPED OUT of the ladies' room, they were greeted by a small, flashily dressed young woman with short, platinum hair and a lightweight camcorder balanced on her shoulder. "Hi there, I'm Karen Schorr from New York 1, it's a pleasure to meet you. You two are interested in future careers in fashion? I love that!" she chattered.

Before Maeve or Katani could even reply, the reporter continued, "All day long I've been looking for an angle that is a little more original than the typical 'girl goes to NYC and makes it big as a model' thing. I mean, BORING, right? Then I'm talking to Michelle and she told me about you two and why you were here and I said 'Shut up!' and she said 'No, I can't, because it's true' and I thought that you would be the perfect interviews, do you know why?"

Katani and Maeve looked as each other and Katani asked nervously, "Um, why?"

"Because our viewers just love stories about proactive young women. Girls who want to get a head start on their careers and who dream big, you know? This is perfect! It'll be right up their alley!"

Both girls stood there not knowing what to do with Karen's super-charged professional energy and nonstop chatter. Katani looked like she had been plowed over with a steamroller. But Maeve, captivated, whispered under her breath, "Someday I want to be just like her …"

Michelle squeezed both girls' shoulders reassuringly. "Excuse me," she said tactfully, "but I have to go tie up a few loose ends before the show. You girls will be just fine." She winked at Katani and Maeve and asked Karen, "Can I help you find a place to set up backstage?"

"That would be great," said Karen. She and the girls followed Michelle to the backstage area, and Michelle led them to an empty corner out of the way of the fashion show hubbub.

"How does this work?" Michelle asked. "I figured it would be quieter than anywhere else."

"Yes. This looks great," Karen said cheerily.

"And you'll want the girls made up for the camera, right?" Michelle turned to Katani and Maeve. "Come with me. I'll get Andre to squeeze you in while Karen's setting up."

"Thanks, Michelle!" Karen called. As they walked away, she pulled a tripod out of her backpack and began to set up the camcorder on it.

"Andre," Michelle said to a man standing behind a makeup chair. He quickly brushed shaggy strands of bleached blond hair out of his eyes and looked up. "I need you to make these two up ASAP. Nothing drastic—just a little powder, blush and lipstick, all right? They're doing a TV interview. And remember, dearest, they're only twelve."

"Michelle!" Katani was mortified.

Andre laughed and kissed Michelle on the cheek. "Only for you, darling," he said, flicking back his hair and nodding for Katani to get into the chair. "Honestly, Michelle, if I hear one more word from one of these stuck-up models about me designing personalized eyeshadow to match the exact shade of their eyes, I will freak out. I'm telling you! This one is missing a shoe, that one has bags under her eyes, blah, blah, blah—I've never seen such unprofessionalism in all my life!" He signed and inspected Katani. "Look at this one! Great skin tone. Hmm. Piece of cake!"

"Excellent. OK, see you soon, girls," and with that, Michelle was off to work. Andre began by wiping Katani's face with a clean sponge and then proceeded to deftly apply foundation to her cheeks, blending it in with his fingers. It seemed like he needed only a few strokes to get the effect he wanted. He dabbed a little more onto her forehead, dotted some on her chin and throat, and then stood back, pleased with his work. Another minute and he had matched a perfect pink hue to Katani's natural cinnamon skin tone and lightly dusted her face with blush.

Katani kept stealing glimpses of herself in the mirror, astounded at what she saw. It wasn't that she looked totally different from how she normally looked. She had the same eyes, nose, hair, and everything. She just looked older somehow, more graceful, and composed. All it took was a few flicks of Andre's wrist—and bam!

Maeve watched, awestruck, as Andre traced the outline of Katani's lips with a subtle lip liner, and then used a shimmery gloss to make it really zing. He handed her a tissue and made a smacking noise with his own lips to demonstrate what she was supposed to do. "Blot it off and it looks just right, yes?" he instructed. "Much better for young ladies. Too much lipstick or dark eyeliner—blugh!"

Katani stared at herself in the mirror. She couldn't believe the transformation. She felt like a princess. At this moment, she could be anyone from a famous fashion designer to a no-nonsense businesswoman! And she *liked* the way she felt!

From a corner of the room they heard, "Will someone please find my shoes before I go completely *mad*?" From another corner one of the girls wailed, "Geri? Where is Geri!? These straps are too tight!"

"This dress ..." growled another girl, "looks absolutely *hideous* on me!"

"All right, your turn, missy," Andre said to Maeve, ignoring the shouts and shrieks around him. Katani slid off the chair and Maeve hopped up obediently. "Love, love, *love* the red hair," Andre enthused as he wiped her face clean and worked in a cream-colored foundation. He picked a soft bubblegum pink powder for her cheecks and glossed her lips with subtle berry.

Andre pointed to the mirror in front of Maeve. "Eh—voilà!" he said with an exaggerated bow. "You like?"

Why was it that when Maeve tried to do her own makeup, it never looked this good? With her red locks cascading around her face, which had been kissed ever-so-slightly with glitter, Maeve thought she looked magical. "Oh, yes!" Maeve said. "I love it! You are so nice to do this."

"Not a problem," Andre answered with a flourish. "Makeup is important in the fashion world, and I think of myself as a painter ... a painter of faces. It's what I do and I love my job ... unless I have to deal with spoiled divas. Rude, rude, rude!"

"Thank you again, Andre," Katani said more formally. She didn't want Andre to think she was an ungrateful diva. Although with all the chaos surrounding the show, Katani could understand how some models might got carried away.

Katani was so overwhelmed with everything that was happening she felt like she might float away. First, she had her makeup done by a real New York City makeup artist, and now here she was about to have a news interview about her dream of a career in fashion—what more could this day have in store?

Karen reappeared, still a tornado of energy. "Done? Yes? Fabulous! You girls look amazing. OK, let's get this show on the road!"

Karen had already set up her camera on the tripod and quickly herded the girls in front of it. She peered through the lens to check the picture. "Just making sure all three of us fit in the frame. There, that's perfect."

She turned on the light, adjusted the angle, and walked in front of the camera with her microphone. The nervous, over-excited energy suddenly disappeared. In a second Karen became low-voiced, level-headed, and more like, in Katani's opinion, a professional reporter. "So you are Katani Summers and you are Maeve Kaplan-Taylor, right? Just checking. This is going to be a short segment, but I'll make sure you get copies, all right? It'll be a nice souvenir to take home. Remember, look at me, not the camera, OK? Good. All right, here's the countdown, girls, ready? Three, two, one …"

Maeve and Katani squeezed hands for good luck as Karen launched into her spiel. "Hello, I'm Karen Schorr from New York 1, and here we are at the *Teen Beat* Magazine Fashion Show. There has been a lot of excitement about this show, as it is the first fashion show sponsored by *Teen Beat*— the magazine of the moment for teen girls across the globe. We will get an exclusive look at debut lines from hot new designers! Plus it's *the* place to see and be seen this afternoon in New York. If you're lucky enough to get past the paparazzi, you'll surely be rubbing elbows with all kinds of exciting

❀

people, including a certain heartthrob all the way from London. But first I have two special young ladies from Boston, Maeve Kaplan-Taylor and Katani Summers." The two girls smiled at the camera. Maeve beamed comfortably and tossed her curls behind her back as she tilted her head to the side. Lights, Camera, Action—she was in her element. Next to her, Katani sat stiff as a board. The tight, nervous grin pasted on her face was very unlike her normal smile.

Karen went on. "These ambitious young girls are interested in careers in the fashion industry. By participating in this show today, they are taking their first steps in that direction. Tell me, ladies, is modeling your first choice?"

Katani looked astonished. Modeling? She wasn't expecting this, and she didn't have a clue how to answer.

Unlike Katani, who sat flabbergasted without a thing to say, Maeve seemed to have plenty of ideas. She didn't even need to think before casually responding, "Good question, Karen. To be honest … no, I'm not planning on becoming a model. I love fashion though! And I think the most exciting part for me … and my career … is just to be at this show in the first place!"

"Oh?" Karen prompted her. "Why?"

"Well, Karen," Maeve went on, "I'm an actress."

"Really?" asked Karen in a fascinated voice.

Really? thought Katani.

"Yes, Karen. I mean, so far I've only done a few independent productions … locally, you know, but eventually I plan on bigger things. Broadway, for instance. Also, Hollywood is another goal of mine. But when you are an actress, it's really important to meet other people in the industry. So it's really exciting that so many famous actors and actresses are here at this show today." Maeve smiled again and repeated her head tilt/hair toss.

Katani could not believe her ears. Maeve *sounded* like a major movie star. Where was all this confidence coming from? She suddenly felt very foolish. Why couldn't she think of anything to say? Had she lost her brain all of a sudden? She was Katani Summers, one of the best students at Abigail Adams Junior High, and she felt like a moron with nothing to say. She began to feel faint.

"Wow, Maeve, you really know what you want! Now let me ask, is there anyone here today that you're especially excited about meeting?"

Katani shifted awkwardly, unsure of where she should be looking. Karen didn't seem to care one bit about talking to her. Katani felt frozen, trying to think of some way to enter the conversation. This was her passion, after all. Karen was completely ignoring the person who came here because of her love of fashion as she chatted away with Maeve … as though they were lifelong friends!

Katani decided to impress Karen by telling her the offbeat designers that she was excited about, but before she could get a word in edgewise, Maeve was at it again. "Hmm, who am I excited about? Well, of course, Simon Blackstone is here, star of *The Swashbuckler*! I've been a fan for a while of course, but today I got to spend some time with him one-on-one and he is really an awesome guy. *Very* down-to-earth."

"Wow, one-on-one with Simon Blackstone. That is exciting," Karen said as though she really meant it. "He's one of my favorites, too. I guess this means it'll be just as much fun watching the audience as it will be watching the runway!"

"Totally!" Maeve agreed. "I know I'll be keeping my eyes peeled in both directions!" She and Karen laughed.

Katani couldn't believe how comfortable Maeve was in

front of the camera. She sounded as though she was having a regular conversation with the BSG back home, instead of talking to a real reporter. *That's her star quality*, Katani thought. *I feel so out of place just standing here …*

When Karen asked Maeve what she was doing to prepare for a stage career, Maeve explained how her father ran the Movie House and how she got to watch movies there all the time. "You can learn so much from the really great, classic actors and actresses. I feel like just sitting with my popcorn in the theater is like getting an education in film!"

"Wow, that's a great way to look at it!" Karen complimented her. "You sound pretty serious about making a big splash someday. Perhaps here in the Big Apple?"

"Well, Karen, maybe you and I will be talking again in a few years," Maeve said with a wink and a warm smile. Katani was astounded and coughed out of shock. How was her friend such a natural?

Karen seemed to remember suddenly that she had another person on camera. She turned to Katani. "Well, Katani, what about you? Do you see floor lights and stage curtains in your future?"

Katani felt her stomach flop as she opened her mouth to speak. "No, no," Katani said, laughing nervously. "I am very interested in fashion. Actually, I want to start my own fashion business someday."

Karen nodded. "Oh?"

Feeling a little looser, Katani continued, "Yes. I'm really excited to be helping backstage at the show this weekend. I'm sure I'm going to learn a lot here about how the fashion world really works—"

"That's great. Well it looks like you girls are right where you need to be!" Karen interrupted.

"Oh yeah!" Maeve gushed.

"Actually I—" Katani was about to explain that she wanted to see the thought processes behind making the clothes, but Karen immediately jumped in.

"Well, that's all the time we have!" she chirped. "We have been hanging out with Maeve Kaplan-Taylor, a girl I'm sure we'll be seeing more of, and Katani Summerville, from Boston. Thank you girls, and have a great time at the show."

Karen waited a few seconds as the girls held their smiles for the camera, then announced, "And—cut! Thanks a million, girls. That's going to be great." In a minute, she had taken the camcorder apart, stored the tripod in its case, and cleaned up the rest of the equipment. She gave the girls a friendly wave as she bustled down the hallway.

Maeve beamed at Katani. "That went well, don't you think?" she asked.

Katani shrugged and looked dazed. "Didn't you hear what happened? She got my name wrong."

"Oh I missed that ..."

"And she barely even talked to me. The whole interview was about you becoming an actress," Katani choked. She didn't mean to let it all slip out like that. She knew she sounded envious but she couldn't help herself. It was her big break and she blew it. No one would ever want to hire her when she grew up if she couldn't even utter a coherent sentence on camera. This was all so upsetting. Katani stifled her tears.

Maeve's smile faded. "I'm sorry, Katani. I ... I don't know what happened. She just started asking me questions ... and I knew the answers. It was so different from school ..."

"I know," Katani admitted, exhaling a deep breath. "It's not you, Maeve. You were awesome. You know just how to talk in front of a camera. I guess that's why you want to be an actress. It's just that since we're at a fashion show, I thought I'd get more of a chance to talk about what was going on here."

"Maybe we can get her to shoot another take?" Maeve suggested optimistically.

"Nah, I guess the thing about news is … they just cover whatever is the most interesting. Besides, that Karen woman is long gone by now."

As Maeve turned to see if there was any trace of the chatty reporter, Michelle suddenly sprinted around the corner. She rushed up to the girls and grabbed Katani's arm. "Thank goodness I found you. We have an emergency!" she said quickly.

"What? What's wrong?" Katani asked, hardly able to stay on her feet as Michelle pulled her through the crowd. Maeve hurried after them. She wasn't about to lose her friends a second time that day.

"Shh—just follow me and act like you know what you're doing." Finally Michelle stopped in front of a short, muscular man with a slick silver ponytail. "Blaze, this is Katani Summers—the girl I was telling you about."

Blaze, with his ponytail gleaming in the makeup mirror and the deliberate wrinkles in his silk shirt, looked every bit the designer. He spun around to inspect Katani. "Stand up straight," he commanded.

Katani stood tall, her expression serious. Blaze lifted his arms and, framing her face with his hands, suspiciously studied Katani. Then he gave a quick, deciding clap and declared, "Yes! You were right, Michelle. She's perfect."

"Perfect for what?" Katani asked hesitantly.

"Blaze needs you to model," Blaze began, starting to assemble skirts and pants suits in a circle at Katani's feet. "One of my models just got sick—perfect timing, right? I need her on the runway and she's in the bathroom moaning, 'Food poisoning! Food poisoning!' Blaze tells these girls a billion times, no seafood on runway days. Then I see this girl eating shrimp cocktail and an hour later, Blaze is calling 911, ambulance, and she has the food poisoning. Well the show must go on, and Blaze needs a replacement."

"But I'm not a model!" Katani gasped. Blaze continued to pull together clothes and accessories, unaffected by Katani's hesitation. "You are now, kiddo. We've got to hustle. People want to see Blaze's designs. We need a model, and you are it!"

"You should do it, K," Michelle whispered. "It'll be a great experience. Think how much you'll learn about fashion from actually being in the show."

"I'm really not sure," Katani started to say.

Maeve popped up behind her. "If you don't want to do it, I wouldn't mind. I'm really comfortable on stage," she said with a wide smile.

Blaze gave her one glance and rolled his eyes. "Blaze does not have time for this ... this ... ridiculousness. Please, people, I need *models* here! Is that too much to ask?" Blaze started hyperventilating and fanning himself with his rumpled shirt.

Maeve seemed to shrink as she looked away. Two patches of red appeared on her cheeks, as though someone had slapped her.

"Hey!" Katani said. "She's my *friend*!"

Michelle's mouth hung open as she tried to find the right words. Maeve breathed deeply as she pushed back the hurt. "It's OK, Katani. You should be the one to do this. You are perfect, so ... I'm just going to get out of the way."

"But—" Katani begin.

"Shhh!!" Maeve made a brushing motion as if to say

✿

forget about it, as she walked away to seek cover from the hurricane of commotion surrounding Katani.

As she spun around to leave, Blaze caught a glimpse of her fiery red locks. "See now this is what Blaze is talking about! The hair, it is gorgeous. You should do shampoo commercials, yes?"

"Are you talking to me?" Maeve asked, running a finger through her hair.

"Yes, you. Too short for the runway, but just right for the shampoo commercials, I think. Very pretty face." Then—just like that—Blaze forgot about Maeve and turned his attention back to Katani.

Bye, Maeve mouthed as she tiptoed away.

Katani wished she didn't feel so alone and overwhelmed as the crowd of strangers swooped in around her.

"Shoe size?"

"Huh?" Katani looked down to see a tiny, elfin-like woman crawling around her feet.

"Hmm—eight or nine?" asked the woman.

"8 ½," Katani answered. They pulled her over to a vacant corner to show her the outfits she would be wearing.

"The gold sweater and skirt first. Get her ready and get her out there!" Blaze started clapping as he shouted, "Move it, move it, move it!"

Maeve found an empty chair in a corner by an unlit mirror. She tried to offer supportive smiles to her friend, but inside she was aching. She couldn't remember the last time she'd been so embarrassed. Even Blaze's compliment about her beautiful red hair didn't take away the sting that they didn't want her to model.

She could feel tears rising in her eyes, but she blinked them away. It was silly to be upset about this. Designers had their needs, she supposed. But it did feel terrible that he had rejected her on the spot. *Maeve, chill out*, she told herself. *It's no big deal.* She looked at her own reflection in the dim mirror. How could she have so quickly forgotten Andre's lovely makeup job? Maeve sniffled away her sadness and gave her best television-worthy smile, remembering how well the interview had gone that morning. Her ego was almost fully recovered when two models approached and sat down on the other side of the mirror. They must have thought they were alone in the dark corner and began to freely gossip as they strapped on high sandals and primped. "Oh my gosh, *here's* a good one! Did you hear about that little girl who asked to model for Blaze?" one voice tittered.

Maeve heard a second voice burst into laughter. "Did I hear about it? Kaloren, I was *there*! It was hilarious! Blaze got so upset … he's so dramatic. I love it," she snorted.

"These kids …" the other girl, apparently Kaloren, huffed. "I mean, they think that you can just walk off the street and magically become a model."

"Well," the second model said knowingly, "we did."

They giggled.

"Whatever. Modeling is one of those things. You've either got it, or you don't and that's just the way it is."

"Totally," the other model said. "How do I look?"

"Hot," answered Kaloren. "Let's go."

Both girls laughed once more, tugged at the straps of their sandals, and trotted off toward the show.

Maeve drew back behind the mirror. Now she was the one who felt sick. They were making fun of her because Blaze hadn't chosen her to model?

"Do I really look all that different from them?" Maeve asked herself as she looked into the three-sided mirror. Back at

school, she was a glamour girl. And of course her hair was exceptional! After all, it was her signature trademark. But Maeve wanted to be able to do whatever she set her mind to. She didn't want to be a shampoo girl, and she certainly didn't want to be mocked by a couple of mean girls—even if they were world-class models.

"There you are. I thought you might have overheard our little friends," said a voice. It was coming from behind another mirror. A woman poked her head out from the side. She was wearing tight leather pants with a matching halter-top. Her blonde hair, which she was in the middle of fixing, was full of little sparkles. She took one look at Maeve's unhappy face. "Ah, you did."

Maeve swallowed. "I just don't have the model look, I guess. Those girls *were* right ... you either have it or you don't."

"Model look, yes. Model height ... no, but darling, take a look at them! Most girls in this world will never be so tall. And that's OK. Listen—what's your name?" the model asked.

"Maeve," she whispered.

"Nice to meet you, Maeve. I'm Mimi. Let me tell you the trick about modeling. It is less about the model and more about the clothes. It doesn't matter so much if these girls are anything special, as long as they have the right bodies to wear the clothes. But you know something? You have gorgeous red hair and lovely eyes, and you are going to be a *knockout*." She saw the doubt on Maeve's face. "Trust me. You really are."

"They made fun of me," Maeve said, hardly able to get the words out. "They thought it was ... stupid that I thought I could model."

"Maeve, who cares! From what I hear, you're going to be a famous actress someday."

Maeve looked up, surprised.

"I saw the interview," Mimi explained with a knowing smile. "You have more to offer … that's obvious."

Maeve tried to look grateful. "Thanks," she mumbled. "Really … I'm fine." But saying that only made her feel worse. As far as acting was concerned, her performance of "fine" was not very convincing.

"I have an idea," Mimi said. She sat on the floor with her legs crossed and patted the ground next to her for Maeve to do the same. Mimi looked like a statue of a Greek goddess, completely still amongst the mayhem.

"Come on, Maeve," Mimi urged. "I only have a few minutes before I'm on stage."

Maeve hesitantly obeyed. She would have felt silly sitting there alone, but if she was with a supermodel it couldn't be that bad.

Mimi closed her eyes and placed her hands on her knees with her palms facing upward. "All right, Maeve, take a deep breath through your nose and feel your tummy expand, and hold it in for about five seconds," she instructed. "Ignore everything going on around you."

Maeve inhaled. It only took a moment for her to forget that she was in the middle of a very busy fashion show.

"Now breathe out through your nose and release all hurtful comments and negative thoughts."

Maeve nodded and grinned. In her imagination, Kaloren and Jamie and all their hurtful comments came out too in the form of toxic green smog.

"Now do it one more time," said Mimi. "Breathe in good energy and breathe out the bad."

Maeve repeated the exercise, smiling to herself.

"There." Mimi opened her eyes. "Feel better?"

"Yeah! I really do," Maeve gushed. "What was that?"

Mimi brushed herself and readjusted her outfit. "Just a little cleansing yoga breathing. It helps me every time I get stressed out. Remember, the trick is not to worry about what other people think about you." Mimi threw back her shoulders and shook out her hair, showering Maeve with glitter. "We're special people Maeve. And pettiness is not worth our time."

"Mimi, out front, now!" called a woman at the edge of the room by the curtains.

"Oops! Gotta go," Mimi said. She gave Maeve a wink and click-clacked toward the exit.

Maeve threw back her shoulders like Mimi and stood as tall as she could. She took one more cleansing yoga breath and indeed felt very refreshed. I must remember to invite Mimi to "An Evening with Maeve," she thought. Kaloren and Jamie, on the other hand, are definitely NOT on the list.

CHAPTER 16

❧

THE RUNWAY, THE PIN,
AND THE WARDROBE

"HEY, WANT TO SEE THE coolest part of my job?" Maeve looked up, startled. It was Michelle. Her eyes were blazing with fury.

"Michelle, what's going on?" Maeve asked. She wondered what she had done to get Michelle mad.

"Just watch," Michelle said as she patted Maeve's arm encouragingly. Maeve crept behind a curtain backstage and peered around the edge. Meanwhile, Michelle, notebook in hand, marched straight up to the two models who had made fun of Maeve just a moment ago.

"Excuse me," said Michelle.

The two models, towering over Michelle, sneered at her. They did not seem happy that she was interrupting their conversation. And from the way they were rolling their eyes, Maeve realized they had no idea who Michelle was.

"Could I have your names, please?" Michelle asked.

"We don't do autographs before the show," one of them snapped haughtily.

Michelle smiled smartly. "Oh, don't worry. I'm *with* the

show," she said. "Names?"

"Kaloren Kraus," said the first, tilting her chin into the air.

"Jamie Finkle," said the second, also tilting her chin.

"Great. OK, Kaloren, Jamie, the good news is you still get to work in the show today. The bad news is, you will never model in a *Teen Beat* fashion show again."

Both girls looked stunned. And furious. "Are you kidding me?" gasped Kaloren. "Why?"

"News spread quickly about your immature comments backstage. Your words were very hurtful. At *Teen Beat* we try to make teens and kids feel happy and good about being themselves. We don't care for attitudes like yours and won't support them." Maeve couldn't believe what she was hearing. "Unfortunately for you, your attitudes just don't fit in here. But you have been paid for the day and I expect you to go out there and be professional!" Michelle gave them a stern look and walked away from the stunned models.

"My agent is going to flip!" Kaloren wailed over the music the DJ just started blaring. "I've just got to learn to keep my mouth shut."

When Michelle returned, she gave Maeve a satisfied smile. "Well that was fun! Hey Maeve, the show is just about to start. Why don't you try to get a seat in the first row? You'll get to see everyone up close ... including Katani! And don't worry about those two girls—they will get other jobs, just not at *Teen Beat*. We don't want models with mean, negative attitudes. It reflects badly on what *Teen Beat* is trying to do."

"OK. Gee ... thanks, Michelle," Maeve said. Michelle really did have a cool job. She couldn't believe Katani's cousin had stuck up for her like that. It made her feel a lot better.

On her way to the front, Maeve glimpsed a young model standing still while a bevy of assistants buzzed around her

❁

like flies. Maeve almost fainted when she recognized the face. It was Katani, and she looked fantastic. She was wearing a clingy gold sweater, a matching knee-length swishy skirt, and high-heeled brown leather boots. *Katani is always beautiful*, Maeve thought, *but today she really looks like a top model*.

Maeve wondered how that outfit would look on her. *Probably not as good. Then again, gold really isn't my color*, she thought as she flung back her luxurious, good-for-shampoo-commercials hair.

Just then, someone tapped Maeve on the shoulder. "Excuse me, miss."

When she turned around and saw who it was, she almost fainted for the second time in a minute. It was Isabel's favorite Latina singer, Dina B! "You are the aspiring actress, yes? The one who came here from Boston?"

"I … I …" Maeve was tongue-tied. She had always prided herself on her star-quality speaking skills and here she was … completely star-stuck! Not only was Maeve talking to Dina B, but Dina B had stopped to talk to *her*! She must have seen the news report, and now she knew Maeve wanted to be an actress.

Then Maeve remembered that Dina B was launching her own line of teen clothes that day. *She must be doing the launch right here at the show*, Maeve thought in amazement. *I can't believe I'm talking to her. Isabel is going to be so jealous!*

Dina had warm, caramel skin, almond-shaped dark eyes, brown hair pulled smoothly into a bun behind her head, and a soft, bright smile. She looked a little worried. "I heard your interview with the reporter from New York 1. You did such a wonderful job! And then when Mimi …" Dina glanced in the direction of the kind, blonde model, "… told me about those nasty models, I was so upset! A girl as smart as you,

you probably know how silly it is to say who can and who can't be models! Besides," Dina added with a wink, "from what I hear, you have other plans."

Maeve couldn't believe how glamorous Dina was in person. She wore a full, flaring printed skirt with a wonderful glistening white cap-sleeved blouse tucked into it. She had a marvelous suede belt laced around her waist and a gorgeous amber choker around her neck.

Maeve also noticed that Dina B was *not* towering over her. In fact, she was only a few inches taller than Maeve. In her full skirt and lacy blouse, Dina reminded Maeve of an old-time movie star, like Vivien Leigh. Maeve thought she looked fantastic.

"What is your name again?" asked Dina B.

"Maeve," she answered.

"Well, it is a pleasure to meet you, Maeve. I'm Dina. Today is actually my first runway show. I'm kind of nervous," Dina admitted.

"Oh yes! My friend Isabel and me … we are really big fans! We read that you had a new line of clothes and that no one had seen them yet. We've been wondering what they would look like," Maeve found herself suddenly gushing.

Dina laughed. "Well, my models are right over there wearing them if you want to check out the new line."

She pointed at a table surrounded by a rainbow of colors. The models swirled around like a kaleidoscope in folds of glitter and silk. Some even had feathered boas! And the most amazing part was that Dina's central color theme was a vibrant, raspberry pink. The models all looked fabulous and whimsical. It's like *Legally Blonde* meets *The Princess Bride*, Maeve thought. This is my dream wardrobe!

"What do you think?" Dina asked with her eyebrows

scrunched together. She seemed genuinely interested in Maeve's opinion.

"Wow! I love it!" Maeve breathed. "Really, these clothes are ..." Maeve laughed as she looked down at her own dazzling pink ensemble, "they're just my style!"

"I thought you might like them!" Dina B exclaimed. "When I saw you on the news, you were so funny and cute. And I then I saw your outfit and I thought to myself, bravo! There's a girl after my own heart."

"Thanks!" said Maeve, turning a little pink herself.

Maeve could pick out Dina B's models in the crowd. They were all curvy, healthy-looking girls, wearing beautifully cut print clothes in bright colors, along with unusual jewelry. They were also the only ones eating. Maeve noticed two of them eating good-sized portions of delicious-looking fruit salad and big glasses of milk. Another one was eating a chicken Caesar salad. It all looked wonderful. Maeve was suddenly really hungry.

"Your models seem to be enjoying the food," Maeve commented to Dina.

The singer/designer nodded. "Of course. That's the way it should be. And I encourage them to. They're growing girls; why shouldn't they eat? The fashion world is changing, you know. WE want to design clothes that make all types of women feel beautiful."

Maeve realized that Dina had very definite ideas on this subject. And it gave her a sense of tremendous relief to hear what Dina was saying. She could see that Dina's models were curvier than the other models in the show, but they looked terrific. And the clothes they wore were striking. In fact, Maeve could imagine herself wearing them. She mentioned that to Dina.

Dina smiled and patted her arm again. "You'd better get out front before they start the show. But you know something? *I* can see you wearing my clothes, too. Listen, let's make a deal. When you go to the premiere of your first movie, call me and I will make you a dress, OK? It'll be my gift," said Dina. She reached into her purse and handed Maeve a card. "Here. This is my personal designer line. Stay in touch, Maeve!" Dina gave Maeve a big smile and waved as she turned to go organize her models.

"Gee, thanks," Maeve managed to squeak out. Dina B asked her—Maeve Kaplan-Taylor—to stay in touch. The BSG would never believe this day. To think, all morning long she had thought her clothes were babyish and that she was not good enough to model clothes. Now Maeve was on top of the world. She couldn't believe that in a city like New York, she'd managed to stand out from the crowd just by being herself. Maeve cast a glance at her reflection in a mirror as she headed for the front. *Ah*, she thought blissfully, *there's no business like show business*!

Maeve wanted to get her seat before the show started. She walked down the steps on the side of the stage and looked around. The runway itself was surrounded with hundreds of chairs. Behind that first row, chairs stretched out in all directions, and every single chair seemed to be taken. She looked around for Michelle, but Michelle was no where to be found. *I'm too late*, Maeve thought. *If I can even get a seat, it'll probably be too far back to see Katani.*

The lights began to dim, and Maeve looked around frantically. Then she thought she heard someone say her name.

She squinted through the crowd, but it had become too dark to see anything.

"Maeve! Over here!" called a deep, British voice. Maeve

caught her breath as she realized the man standing and waving from the first row, right in the middle of the runway, was Simon! And there was no doubt about it—he was waving at *her*!

She waved back, trying to seem as cool as possible, and weaved her way through the crowd to him and Bea. They had saved her the seat between them. "Michelle asked us to look after you," Simon whispered as she finally sank down in the chair, "After all, we did a pretty good job last time."

Maeve could hardly speak. She was so overwhelmed by the amazing view and the fantastic company, she felt like laughing out loud. Could this really be happening? Could she, Maeve Kaplan-Taylor, be sitting next to a movie star in the front row of a major fashion show in New York? Wait until Avery, Charlotte, and Isabel heard about this!

"Oh, Maeve, I want you to meet my friend," said Bea, "Rini, this is Maeve. And Maeve, you're from Boston, right?"

Maeve nodded. "Yes, well, actually I live in Brookline. It's one of the suburbs—" Maeve stopped short when she saw the young woman sitting on the other side of Bea. The "Rini" she was about to meet was none other than *the* Rini Miller, one of her favorite teen stars! Could this day get any crazier?

Bea smiled. "Fabulous! Well I'd like you to meet Rini Miller. Rini is going to Boston to shoot a music video next month. Since you are from Boston, I thought maybe you could show her around a little when she gets there. Being a kid in a new city is hard if you don't have a fun person around who knows all the hot places!"

"Of course!" Maeve said. "I'd be happy to! Nice to meet you, Rini."

"Nice to meet you too," said Rini in a quiet voice. "Do you really live near Boston?" she asked Maeve. Rini looked every bit the teen star, with layered blonde hair and a few freckles scattered over a button nose. But when she smiled at Maeve, she seemed really sincere. Maeve liked her on the spot.

"Yup," Maeve said. "I've lived there a long time."

"Wow, that's so cool! I've traveled around a lot, but I've never really lived outside of Idaho. I'm a little nervous about going to Boston. Big cities still kind of scare me!"

"Don't be nervous! Boston is a piece of cake once you get used to it. I think you'll like it!" Maeve said, her natural warmth returning. "My friends in Boston are really nice and we always do lots of fun things. Maybe we could all get together and hang out while you're in the city? We could take you to Montoya's Bakery. They have the yummiest hot chocolate in the world."

"Oh, I'd love that!" Rini cried. "I just hate hanging around in hotel rooms with all the grownups that manage my career. It's so boring. I was worried about feeling like a stranger in Boston. Look, do you mind if I take your number? I'll call you as soon as I know for sure when I'm coming."

Bea smiled and supplied a sheet of paper from a notepad in her purse, and Maeve wrote down her number and email address for Rini. "There's so much to see and do, not only in Boston but in Brookline," she said. "If you're interested, we can take you on a tour of our favorite places when you're done shooting."

"Thanks, I can't wait," Rini said, and she stuffed the paper in to her tiny sparkly purse.

"Shh," Bea said. "I think it's show time."

Techno music began pulsating from the DJ's speakers next to the stage. The room went completely black for a moment, and then the stage became a multicolored light show. The DJ cranked up the volume and as he did, a shower of glitter confetti fluttered down. The curtains slid open and the first model strutted down the runway.

The letters B-L-A-Z-E glowed in a purple light on the backdrop of the stage. Maeve tried not to grin when she saw Kaloren and Jamie, the two models who'd been so rude to her, parading down the catwalk. They moved beautifully and did everything they were supposed to do to show off the clothes they wore, but each had a tight, angry expression. Maeve sighed and thought to herself, *I guess there will always be Queens of Mean wherever I go.*

Since she was right in the front row, both models saw her as they did their slow, graceful saunter down the runway. Kaloren pressed her lips tightly together and shot her a nasty look. Maeve, eager to see Katani, didn't care one bit.

Simon looked bewildered. "I like it when models smile on the runway. Those two look like they've each swallowed a lemon, or something. Blagh!"

Maeve started to giggle and for a minute, she couldn't stop. If Kaloren and Jamie had any idea what they were missing, they'd want to be in the audience too, laughing with movie stars.

There was a rustling next to her, and Maeve turned to see Rini slipping into Bea's seat. "Hope you don't mind," she whispered. "I just have a feeling we'll have a lot to talk about, and Bea didn't mind switching."

Maeve mouthed a thank-you at Bea, who smiled at her, while Rini stared, also perplexed, at Jamie and Kaloren as they turned and started back. "I wouldn't buy those outfits for anything," she declared. "If they make your face all sour like that, why would you want to wear them?"

Maeve laughed out loud. She had a feeling that Rini and all the BSG were going to get along great!

The music picked up and more confetti fell to introduce the final Blaze model, who was wearing the masterpiece outfit of his line. Wild applause erupted at the sight of the stunning young model in sparkling gold fabric. There was Katani, standing frozen on the stage. As Katani took her first steps on the catwalk, Maeve noticed that she seemed a little stiffer than usual. Katani seemed to be looking for someone in the dark sea of the audience. Maeve, sitting front and center, held up her hand and cheered louder than anyone. "Yeah Kgirl! Work it! Work it!"

Katani's uptight expression instantly melted into radiant relief. She was familiar enough with that loud voice to pick it out of any crowd. Katani's steps grew a little more fluid and soon her walk had the mark of regal confidence that the Kgirl was famous for. Katani looked fantastic, and as she got closer and closer to Maeve, her attitude became more and more fantastic as well.

Maeve whispered to Rini, "That's Katani. She's one of my best friends. Blaze put her in the show at the last minute." By the time Katani reached the seats where Simon, Bea, Rini, and Maeve sat, she was walking like a pro, lightly balanced on her high boots, sure of herself and smiling from ear to ear. She looked amazing! Maeve applauded until her palms stung, and Rini did too.

"Your friend is a great model," Rini said to Maeve when Katani had made the long walk back up the runway and disappeared behind the curtain.

"I know! There's just nothing Katani can't do," Maeve said loyally. "If you think she looks good wearing *those* clothes, you should see the things that she designs. Katani wants to start her own fashion business someday."

"Ladies and gentlemen!" blared the loudspeakers.

"There will now be a ten-minute intermission. When we return, you'll be getting the first look at the fantastic new line from the one and only, the great Dina B!"

"Ooh, I'll be right back! I'm going to go see Katani!" Maeve jumped up and stuffed her bag underneath her seat. "Rini, would you mind keeping an eye on this for me? I just have to go back and make sure she's OK."

Rini smiled, "Yeah, no problem. Tell her good job for me!"

Maeve hurried backstage and gasped. If she'd thought it was busy there before, now it was bedlam!

Beautiful clothes were haphazardly thrown everywhere. Models were being zipped, buttoned, and strapped into new outfits in a tornado of motion. The designers screamed wildly about accessories gone missing, scarves draped "all wrong," and skirts fitting improperly. *Even though I'm not always neat*, Maeve thought to herself, *I'd hate being in the middle of all this craziness every day!*

She found Katani already back in her old clothes, lacing up her sneakers. Unlike the other models, Katani had not carelessly thrown anything she'd taken off. Her skirt hung neatly on a special hanger. Maeve was certain Katani's clothes could be worn again without even being ironed!

Katani's eyes lit up when she saw Maeve. "You're here!" She cried as she gave her friend a tight hug. "How'd I do?" Katani asked.

"You were unbelievable!" Maeve told her. "Katani, I swear, you really looked like a model! I think that you could be modeling *right now*?!"

Katani shuddered. "No, thanks! Once was fun, I guess, but it's way too stressful."

"How so?" Maeve asked.

Katani laughed and waved an arm around at all the

shouting and chaos. "I would never be able to handle this! Absolutely, definitely not for me. No, I guess Kelley was right. Fashion, fashion that's my passion. *Designing* fashion, that is!"

"Well, then, it was a great idea to model, wasn't it?" Maeve said practically. "Because now you know you don't want this side of the fashion business."

Katani looked at her, surprised. "You know, you're right. Michelle did me a *big* favor by letting me see this. It seems like some girls get so caught up in the whole dream of becoming a model and they don't get a chance to see what it is actually like."

"Oh, no!" cried a familiar voice. Maeve turned. With her hands placed on her head in anguish, Dina B was walking around in circles, looking like she was going to cry.

"Dina!" Maeve rushed to her side and asked gently, "What happened?"

The designer just pointed. "Look—"

One of her models stood nearby, also looking tragic. She wore a pair of stunning magenta capri pants with a matching top. The only problem was the matching top was soiled with a big, wet blob of coffee from her neck to her waist. It was completely ruined. Dina B's show started in only a few minutes, and one of the models was covered in coffee!

"Oh!" Maeve said woefully. "Dina … do you have an extra shirt that would work?"

Dina shook her head. Tears rose in her eyes. "No … I planned the whole thing perfectly so the girls wouldn't get confused." Dina placed her head in her hand. "And I wanted today to be perfect," she whispered. "This is my first show."

Katani was surveying the disaster a little more hopefully. Maeve could see the sparkle of creativity in her best friend's eye. "Got it!" Katani exclaimed. "Wait just a minute—I think

I can help." And with that she was off.

Dina B looked confused and overwhelmed. "Don't worry!" Maeve assured Dina, comforting the famous singer as she would any friend in need. Maeve continued, "My friend's a great designer. Katani always comes through in a pinch. Just give her a minute, OK?"

"Hey Dina?" It was Michelle, who was also looking tense. "We have a little problem. Even if Katani can fix this, we have to put the whole show on hold. Right now, the stage is empty. It'll be dead space out there! We've got to keep this crowd entertained, so they don't notice."

"Hey, I think I might have an idea!" Maeve said excitedly. "Just tell me, Michelle—what's the deal with your music and sound system?"

"Our guy Grant is running it—he can do anything," Michelle said, looking a little surprised at the question. "It's a sweet idea, Maeve, but I'm not sure if just music is going to cut it—"

"Perfect!" Maeve cried. "That's all I need to know!"

She sprinted away from the chaos and back into the audience again. When she reached Simon, however, she didn't return to her seat. Instead, she took a deep breath, smiled, and said sweetly, "Simon, I have a little favor to ask you …"

A minute later, Michelle was having a quick chat with Grant and an even quicker chat with the show emcee as Maeve crept back to her seat. The lights came down again, and the emcee spoke through his microphone.

"And now, ladies and gentlemen, a very special performance from one of England's most popular stars. Unlike the models, he's not here to show off his clothes, so he asks that you please not look too hard at them." The audience laughed at this as the emcee continued, "Please welcome *The Swashbuckler* himself!"

The familiar beat of Simon's biggest hit blared out of the amplifier as a dry ice machine released a low stream of mysterious fog. The fog began to clear to reveal the dashing Simon Blackstone standing in the middle of the runway.

The audience, surprised at his appearance, cheered madly. Maeve was clapping as hard as she could. How great was it that Simon was willing to get up on stage on a moment's notice to help out the fashion show?

"Come on," Simon shouted, "you all know this one!" And everyone did—not only could everyone sing along, they could dance to it, too ...

KATANI TO THE RESCUE

"Now, just hold still a minute," Katani said to Dina B's model as she fiddled with a pin. Katani was working with one of her own oversized hand-painted scarves that she had brought in her purse. She had selected an electric orange scarf that perfectly complimented the model's pink capris.

"I can't believe it." Dina was astonished. "I think this scarf makes the pants zing even more than before!"

Katani blushed but didn't say a word as she draped the scarf over the model, tying the top two pieces like a halter, and securing the bottom two pieces carefully with safety pins. It took her a while to get it right, but from the sound of it, the audience didn't seem to notice the lag. Everyone backstage could hear the music and the huge commotion going on out front. It sounded like they were dancing out there!

"Hmm ..." Dina murmured as she inspected the model. "I love the scarf, but is there anything we can do to get rid of that droop at the top?" It was true that the scarf was drooping a little, right near the collar. "You can't put a safety pin on the front! And the only kind of jewelry I have with me are necklaces and bracelets. They won't help."

What kind of pin would hold the scarf and still look like it was added on purpose? Katani wondered. "Wait a minute," she said. "I think I might have just the thing!"

She rushed back to her purse and retrieved the horse pin Kelley had given her. She had worn it the whole time, as promised, only taking it off for the fashion show.

"That's adorable!" Dina cried when she saw it. "I've been looking everywhere for interesting pins. Wherever did you get this?"

Katani smiled. "Actually, my sister made it," she answered proudly as she fastened the clay horse to the scarf.

It worked. Everything worked. Models and designers were impressed at the new outfit Katani had cobbled together. They nodded in approval.

"Well, you come from a very artistic family," Dina told Katani. "What talent!"

This was the second time in less than a day that Katani had seen compliments flying over fashion accessories she didn't think were all that special. *I obviously have a lot more to learn than I realized,* she thought to herself.

Out front, Simon was dancing on the catwalk. His dancing was contagious. In a few minutes, the entire first row of the audience was on its feet and dancing too.

Maeve loved this song of Simon's. The lyrics were really catchy with a beat that was impossible not to dance to. After all, this was the song that had made Simon a star. It didn't take her more than a minute to start going wild.

Maeve felt someone elbow her and turned to see Rini. "Wow, Maeve! You're awesome! Where did you learn how to dance like that?"

"Um, I take hip-hop classes," she answered humbly without skipping a beat.

Rini studied Maeve for a moment. When she started to dance again she was following Maeve's snappy moves to a tee. The girls began rocking out in synch, and Maeve laughed out loud—she felt like she was in a music video.

I am dancing with a famous pop star! Maeve thought to herself. *It does not get better than this.* Maeve looked up at the stage and her eyes met Simon's. Grinning, he nodded right at her … and winked. Maeve had to pinch herself to make sure she wasn't dreaming. *OK, I was wrong. THIS is the ultimate! If only the BSG could see me now!*

As the music faded, the singing of the audience melted into applause. Simon was brilliant, sighed Maeve. After he blew kisses into the crowd, he gracefully jogged off stage.

The announcer's voice blared through the loudspeakers. "Thank you, once again to Simon for his impromptu half-time performance! And now … back to the show!"

In a moment Simon Blackstone appeared back in the audience, a little out of breath and dabbled in sweat, but grinning proudly.

"Well done!" Bea whispered.

"You saved the day!" Maeve said gratefully.

"By the way …" she heard Simon say quietly. "Nice dancing, girls."

She and Rini glanced at each other and giggled. Rini seemed just as flattered as Maeve.

A huge disco ball speckled lights across the catwalk as the voice of the announcer began, "Ladies and gentlemen, our next artist is also a musical star in her own right, but this is her official debut as a fashion designer! Let's hear it for the great Dina B!"

There was more applause as Dina confidently strolled to the end of the runway. She stood to one side holding a microphone and showing the audience her pearly smile. "Thank you," she said. "I'm very excited about finally contributing to the fashion world. And we have a beautiful new collection of clothes to show you!"

The models began their graceful parade down the catwalk, with Dina describing the outfits and accessories worn by each.

Dina made sure that the stage had cleared before the final model came out. "This last outfit is something brand new," Dina said finally. "It's not exactly the outfit I planned to show you—but I'm beginning to learn that in every fashion show, not everything goes according to plan!" There was a wave of appreciative laughter, and she went on. "I was fortunate to have the assistance of a terrific young designer you'll all be hearing more from in the future—Katani Summers. So here's my skirt and Katani's hand-painted scarf—an outfit I'm now calling 'Improvisation!'"

When Katani heard Dina's announcement, she gasped. She had tiptoed around the stage and was standing against the wall with the rest of the latecomers. From across the dark crowd she could just make out Maeve's face. They made eye contact and Maeve smiled. *Wow! It was so nice of Dina to give me credit!* Katani thought. *And how amazing to have my design in a major fashion show! This is definitely the very best moment of my life!*

The model did a fabulous, slinky walk down the catwalk. She was confident with her shoulders fixed and her head held high. A wave of applause roared in her ears. There was no doubt about it—the outfit was a smash success!

Katani heard a woman next to her whisper, "I must get that for my Buffy. She would look divine …"

Katani was positively tickled. Oh boy. Life does not get better than this, Katani thought. At least not when you're 12 ...

The rest of the show went by in a blur for both Maeve and Katani. An hour and a half later, the last designer had shown off his last outfit, and the announcer thanked everyone for coming and reminded them of how they could order all the wonderful fashions they had seen that day.

When Maeve and Katani finally managed to squeeze their way backstage, Michelle was standing by the entrance waiting for them. She looked ten times less frazzled and ten times more excited than she had before. She grabbed both of them at once and cried, "Maeve and Katani, I am so proud of you! You two stole the show!"

"I never had more fun in my whole life!" Maeve gasped.

"Me too," Katani agreed. "I'm ready to move to New York right now! Michelle, did you know there are people who already want to buy the outfit I helped Dina put together?"

"I'm not surprised," Michelle said, "I've always known you had style, Katani, but the truth is, I didn't know until today how really talented you are. If you can save a major designer's first collection with a big scarf and a handful of safety pins, I can't even imagine what you'll be able to do when you have a collection of your own."

Katani's eyes glistened. "I can't wait for that day!"

Michelle laughed. "Well, I'm sure you'll find plenty to keep you busy until then. I think this calls for a celebration. Right now. At Serendipity."

The girls looked puzzled. "What's that?"

Michelle stared at them like they each had two heads. "You've never heard of Serendipity—the famous café on the Upper East Side?" Michelle asked. The girls looked at each other, shrugged, and shook their heads. "Well you are in for

❀

171

a treat! Give me about twenty minutes to clean up, and then I'm going to buy you the best frozen hot chocolate you've ever tasted!"

Katani and Maeve exchanged glances. "Better than Montoya's, you think?" Maeve said in a low tone to Katani.

"I doubt it," Katani answered, "but don't tell Michelle. Let's just pretend it's amazing no matter what."

And because they'd both had a rather ridiculous day filled with too many highs and too many lows, Katani and Maeve started to giggle. Pretty soon they were laughing hysterically, leaning on each other for support—right in the middle of the biggest fashion show in New York.

CHAPTER 17

ᲜᲝ

OOPS!

IT WAS GETTING LATE. Isabel had finished her sketch and tucked it neatly in her sketchbook over twenty minutes ago.

"We really should go ..." warned Charlotte.

"OK, let me check and see if Danny the glue boy is still out there."

"Ave—that's the kind of name that could haunt Danny for the rest of his middle school life," Charlotte said sharply.

"Sorry, but geesh, could that guy get a life?" Avery replied. Charlotte shook her head. That comment was so Avery.

Isabel looked up with a start. "What's that noise?" She heard what sounded like heavy footsteps coming right toward the storage room. "Is it Danny?"

"Not sure." Avery bent to peer through the keyhole. "Oh no!" she said breathlessly, "He's coming this way. Hide!"

Charlotte and Isabel ducked behind a display case. Avery crouched under a table. For a moment none of them breathed.

They waited for Danny's voice to ask them if they were OK. Instead, they heard nothing but the sound of heavy footsteps clumping *into* the room. There was a loud grunt, as

✿

the overhead lights snapped off. Then—SLAM.

"Was that the door?" Charlotte whispered. The three sat in silence to the worst sound of all: a key scraping in the lock. The footsteps receded. In a moment everything was quiet again.

Finally, Avery spoke. "Hello? Anybody here?"

"Of course we're here," Isabel whispered back. "But now we're locked in! What are we going to do?"

"It'll be all right," Charlotte said calmly. "Let's start by turning the lights back on."

She inched out of her hiding place behind the display case and began to move cautiously around the room, concentrating hard to remember where each object and piece of furniture was placed so she didn't bump into anything. She groped her way to the light and flicked the switch. It didn't do much.

"Can you turn on more lights, Char?" Avery asked urgently. "I still can't see a thing!"

Charlotte tried, but shook her head. "There's only one set of switches in here. The rest of the lights are probably on the museum timer. They must just turn off automatically."

Isabel gulped. In the darkness she had no idea what kind of scary old things were around her. "I'm getting really creeped out in here," she said in a low voice.

Suddenly they heard a voice. It was so unexpected that all three girls jumped.

The voice was coming from a loudspeaker that was being broadcasted into the room. "Good afternoon. The Museum of Fine Arts will be closing in 15 minutes. Please make your way to the museum lobby to pick up your coats and personal belongings before you leave. Thank you very much for visiting the Museum of Fine Arts today."

"15 minutes?!" Charlotte exclaimed. "Should we yell for

help? We could be in here all night!"

"No—don't yell!" Isabel pleaded. "If Danny's still outside the door, he's going to hear us!"

"Izzy, we have to let someone know we're here," Avery insisted. "If it's Danny, well, that's too bad. I don't want to be stuck here all night. If you want to hide from him, you can climb into a mummy case … just kidding."

Charlotte started to giggle and then stopped. She gasped. Isabel crawled out from behind the case and asked, "What is it, Char?"

Charlotte nodded toward the wall. The mummy case that had been firmly closed when they came in was now cracked open.

All three girls froze.

Isabel began to breathe hard. "This is bad. This is very, very bad."

Charlotte tried to stay calm. "Maybe it was open when we came in. We just thought it was closed."

Isabel's eyes grew wider. "Or maybe it opened by itself—by some evil force that lives inside."

"Come on, Izzy," Avery said, trying to be brave. "It's a mummy case, not a magic lamp. I promise it's not haunted."

"HAUNTED? I just thought there was a force. I didn't even think of *haunted*!" Isabel said, breathing harder and harder. Unable to stand still, she began to pace in a small circle around the table, careful to keep the table between her and the open mummy case. "Maybe this room is haunted—it's been so full of dead people and their things for so long—maybe they really *do* come back to life—how does anyone know for sure?"

"Those are just movies, Isabel," Charlotte said, trying to sound reassuring. "Nothing like that is going to happen here."

"Who knows what happens when the museum closes?" Isabel cried, talking faster and faster. "When all the guards and tour guides and cleaning crews leave, who knows what happens?"

Isabel's words were so full of fear that Avery and Charlotte were getting freaked out too. "Maybe Isabel's right," Charlotte said timidly. "I mean, when everybody goes home—who knows?"

"That's silly," Avery scoffed. But her heart was pounding harder than it had when she'd played a full hour of soccer without stopping.

For a minute the room was silent except for the heavy breathing of all three girls, who were getting more frightened by the minute.

Suddenly, the amulet Isabel had been sketching fell off the table with a *crash*.

That did it.

Isabel, Charlotte, and Avery rushed to the door of the storage room and pounded on it as hard as they could. "HELP! Somebody! LET US OUT!" they screamed over and over at the top of their lungs.

CHAPTER 18

CR

KNOCK, KNOCK! WHO'S THERE?

"WHAT IF WE DON'T GET OUT TONIGHT?" Isabel gasped, trying to find enough breath to yell again. "Ms. Rodriguez is going to be so mad!"

"So is Mrs. Fields …" Charlotte added. The girls looked at one another.

"OK, we have to yell louder. One more time—" Isabel inhaled deeply, ready to shriek again.

"Shh! Hold on!" Avery said. She pressed her ear against the door.

There were footsteps—lots of footsteps. It sounded like they were headed right toward them!

"OK, now!" Avery commanded. They began yelling again.

"Help! We're in here … we're in the storage room! Somebody! We're locked in!"

Suddenly there was a banging on the door and a yell from the other side, "Calm down, kids! We hear you! Just give us a second to get in there."

The lock began to tremble and then turned. Light hit their faces as the storage room door was finally pulled open!

Isabel was so anxious to get away from the open mummy case that she threw herself against the door just as the security guards opened it. The door flew open and sent Isabel, stunned, flying headlong into the hallway.

Luckily, on the way to the marble floor, someone caught her fall with a startled "Oof!" and steadied Isabel on her feet.

"Sorry," she gasped. "But I had to get away from those mummies!"

She looked up gratefully into the face of her rescuer.

Oh, *no*. It was Danny. Isabel didn't remember Danny being this tall.

"Are you OK, Isabel?" Danny asked.

"Yes. I am fine, thank you," Isabel said with a tight smile. She nodded at Danny and took a step back to where Avery and Charlotte were standing, trying their best to keep straight faces. Oh just my luck, Isabel thought to herself. But at least Danny is alive and not some *thing* that came back from the dead.

The girls smiled gratefully at the two guards who had unlocked the door. "Thank you so much!" Isabel said.

Charlotte nodded. "Yeah! But how did you know we were here?" she asked.

"It's this young man you should be thanking," one of the guards said, patting Danny on the shoulder. "If it wasn't for him, you girls might have been stuck there all night. Good thing he happened to be walking by the ladies' room, and heard you yelling. He alerted the museum staff right away."

"That's funny," Avery said. "What were you doing by the ladies' room, Danny? There isn't even any art in this hall. Boy, I guess we did luck out!"

Danny turned beet red. Isabel had to stifle a laugh.

"Oh, no!" Charlotte nudged her friends. They looked up to see Ms. Weston charging down the hall. Following behind her was not only the museum docent, but half the kids on their field trip, several chaperones ... and Ms. Rodriguez!

Anna and Joline were huddled together giggling. "This is *too* funny," they heard Anna whisper to Joline.

Ms. Rodriguez looked more upset than they'd ever seen her. "We've been looking everywhere for you girls!" she said. "I have been worried sick!" Ms. R clasped her chest. Her eyes were full of disappointment.

"We didn't mean to get locked in," Avery mumbled. "We were just trying to—"

"Enough," Ms. Rodriguez said. She stared at her students, lingering on Anna and Joline, who suddenly got very quiet. "Avery, Charlotte, Isabel—we'll discuss this *in private*. Follow me. Ms. Weston, why don't you come along as well? We'll meet the rest of you at the bus." No matter how upset Ms. Rodriguez was, she would never create a scene about something like this in front of the whole class.

Isabel felt especially guilty as they made their way down the museum corridor away from the rest of the students. All she wanted was to get away from Danny without hurting his feelings. The problem was he just wouldn't take the hint. Isabel felt like a fool for running away from Danny all afternoon. And things had escalated and escalated. Maybe if she'd let Avery and Charlotte yell when they wanted to, right after they first got locked in, they could have been rescued without Danny's help.

Ms. Weston, who was walking next to Ms. Rodriguez, looked back at Isabel. "This isn't like you, Isabel. Or you two, either," she said to a red-faced Charlotte and Avery. "I think there's more to this, Ms. Rodriguez. We ought to hear the whole story before we come to any major conclusions."

"I'd like to think that you girls would know better," Ms.

Rodriguez added.

Charlotte, Avery, and Isabel glanced at each other. Ms. Rodriguez looked serious but not cross, and was going to hear the girls' side of the story before she made any decisions.

Ms. Rodriguez gestured for everyone to stop as soon as she found a quiet corner. "All right girls. What happened?"

"It's all my fault, Ms. Rodriguez," Isabel blurted. "Avery and Charlotte were only trying to help."

Isabel told the two teachers how Danny followed her around all over the museum and bothered her whenever she tried to sketch or enjoy the artwork on her own. "We didn't *mean* to hide in the storage room, but we didn't know how else to lose him. I know it was wrong," Isabel admitted. "I'm really sorry."

"I'm sorry too," said Charlotte.

"Me too," added Avery.

"How come you didn't just tell Danny you needed your space?" asked Ms. Weston.

Isabel shrugged and said in a soft voice, "I tried to let him know, but he just didn't take the hint. I guess I should have said something stronger but I didn't want to hurt his feelings."

"Hmm ..." Ms. Weston looked at Ms. Rodriguez. "There really isn't an easy way to deal with that type of thing."

"No, I suppose we haven't covered that," Ms. Rodriguez agreed. She too was thinking deeply. "You know, Isabel, if anyone is ever bothering you, even if it doesn't seem like that big of a deal, it is very important for you to let him know that you need your space. If you are afraid of hurting his feelings just say, 'I don't want to be rude, but I want to be left alone right now.' Usually that's all it takes. If it doesn't work, please come and talk to a chaperone, like Ms. Weston or myself. That's what we're here for. Besides, it's much better than hiding out in a storage room." She smiled.

"Danny didn't mean to do anything wrong, but I should have been more clear I guess," Isabel said. "I'm sorry we ran off and hid like that, Ms. Rodriguez. That was a big mistake."

"Ms. R, I don't think Danny is the type of kid to take a hint." Avery leaned in conspiratorially to Ms. Rodriguez. "Danny is a real talker, Ms. R, and he just loves to show off how much he knows."

"That may be true," Ms. R agreed. "But I think it's always a better choice than running off and hiding, right?"

"If a mummy is chasing you …" Avery didn't have time to even finish her sentence. Ms. R's expression meant the discussion was over.

"Would you like me to have a talk with Danny?" Ms. Weston asked Isabel.

"Umm …" Isabel hesitated.

"I'll tell you what," Ms. Weston began. "Why don't I have a little chat with him after school about what the signs are that someone wants to be left alone? As long as you just give him a friendly word now and then, I think everything will be fine."

"Not *too* friendly!" Avery whispered to Charlotte.

Ms. Rodriguez tried to be stern again. "So is this the last time you girls will ever run off on a class trip?"

"The LAST," Avery promised.

"Definitely," Charlotte agreed.

"*Never again*," Isabel stressed.

"All right then, girls. Charlotte, I'm confident that your time with the exhibits is going to provide some great material for you to write about in *The Sentinel*."

Charlotte began to smile. "I hope so," she said.

"And *I'm sure* that we will be seeing lovely artwork from

you, Isabel?"

"Totally!" Isabel assured her, thinking of her sketches from the storage room.

"Well, then I'm glad that you got something out of it. But don't—and I mean don't—" Ms. R said with a twinkle in her eye,"—let it happen again!"

Ms. R looked at her watch. "OK, let's go, kids. We're already running twenty minutes late."

As soon as they exited the museum and were settled on the bus with the rest of the group, Ms. R signaled the driver to start, and the big yellow bus began rattling toward Brookline.

The three girls huddled together in their seat. "What a day!" Charlotte said. "Do you think Maeve and Katani had any adventures in New York City?"

"Compared to us? Hah! Impossible," Avery declared. "Wait'll they hear about this! They're going to be extremely sorry they missed 'The Case of the Mummy Who Came Back from the Dead.'"

"I'm not so sure," Isabel said with a grin. "I would have been OK with missing being stalked by Danny AND by mummies all in one day!"

"What Danny needs," Charlotte said thoughtfully, "is someone else to have a crush on, other than Isabel. You know, someone who can appreciate his ..." she coughed, "his finer qualities." Her eyes gleamed.

Betsy Fitzgerald, who was sitting in the bench behind them, was bent earnestly over a huge coffee-table-sized book about Egypt in her lap. Even on the bus, she wasn't missing a chance to study. "Hmm ..." Avery tapped her chin. "Does the word 'soul-mate' ring a bell?"

Both Charlotte and Isabel, following her gaze, covered their mouths as they burst out laughing.

CHAPTER 19

❧

THE CORE OF THE BIG APPLE

THOUGH KATANI AND MAEVE LOVED the hot chocolate from Montoya's Bakery, they had to agree that Serendipity's "Frrrozen Hot Chocolate" was a scrumptious experience. Maeve pronounced it to be "among the finer things in life."

They left Serendipity's full of sugar and completely exhausted in the best way you can be tired after a day jam-packed with incredible surprises. When Maeve and Katani returned to Michelle's apartment, they also agreed that they had to tell the rest of the BSG about their incredible day, although they wouldn't reveal *everything* until they came home. "I can't wait to see the look on their faces when I tell them about how I asked Simon to dance," Maeve pointed out. "*And* being interviewed on TV!"

"And I want to tell them in person about how I helped Dina B," Katani added.

Maeve noticed that Katani didn't mention modeling in the show as a highlight. Until today, Maeve would have thought that modeling was the coolest part of the fashion show. But Katani didn't see it as all that important; she was proud that people actually appreciated her design talents.

Before they could get on the computer and IM the other BSG, Michelle noticed the light flashing on her answering machine. "Better wait a minute," she joked. "It could be *Vogue* asking Katani to do a layout for them, or maybe it's Simon Blackstone's record company trying to sign Maeve onto their label!"

In fact, it was Maeve's father. "Hi, Maeve," the message began. "Slight change of plans. Turns out Grandma and Grandpa have tickets for a show tomorrow, so they won't be around. I thought it would be fun to take Sam and you and Katani to Ellis Island to do some sightseeing. That's where most European immigrants entered New York, you know. It should be very educational ..." Maeve winced at the word "educational." But Mr. Taylor continued, "... AND fun. So I'll pick you up tomorrow at ten, OK? Maybe we can even do some shopping later." Katani's face lit up at the mention of shopping. "See you tomorrow, honey," Mr. Taylor said. "I hope you had some time for fun today. Those fashion shows can be a lot of work! OK, love you. Bye!"

When the message ended, Maeve and Katani glanced at each other and burst out laughing.

"Come on," Maeve said. "I absolutely can't wait another second. We have to tell the girls what happened today."

"Not everything!" Katani reminded her.

"Not everything," Maeve agreed. "Just enough so they'll be dying to hear more!"

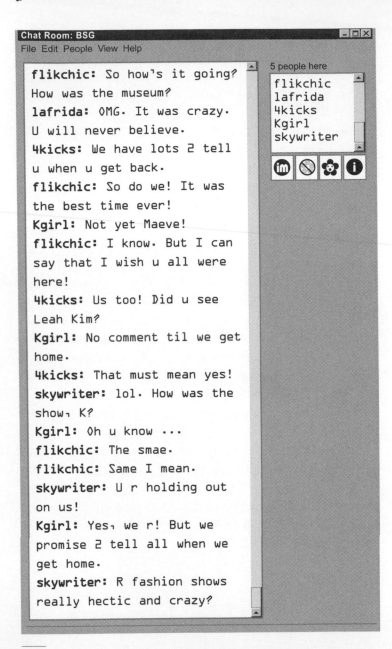

flikchic: So how's it going? How was the museum?

lafrida: OMG. It was crazy. U will never believe.

4kicks: We have lots 2 tell u when u get back.

flikchic: So do we! It was the best time ever!

Kgirl: Not yet Maeve!

flikchic: I know. But I can say that I wish u all were here!

4kicks: Us too! Did u see Leah Kim?

Kgirl: No comment til we get home.

4kicks: That must mean yes!

skywriter: lol. How was the show, K?

Kgirl: Oh u know ...

flikchic: The smae.

flikchic: Same I mean.

skywriter: U r holding out on us!

Kgirl: Yes, we r! But we promise 2 tell all when we get home.

skywriter: R fashion shows really hectic and crazy?

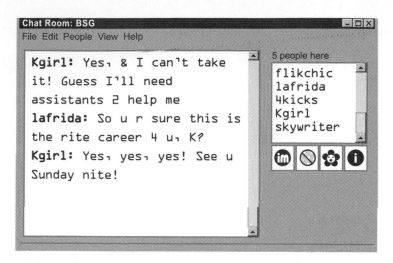

Chat Room: BSG
File Edit People View Help

Kgirl: Yes, & I can't take it! Guess I'll need assistants 2 help me
lafrida: So u r sure this is the rite career 4 u, K?
Kgirl: Yes, yes, yes! See u Sunday nite!

5 people here

flikchic
lafrida
4kicks
Kgirl
skywriter

A NAME ON THE WALL

Mr. Taylor arrived promptly at 10 o'clock on Saturday. Katani and Maeve were waiting for him.

That morning Maeve's tendency to be messy didn't bother Katani one bit. Maeve was such a good friend, so loyal and fun. Katani couldn't blame her for not being neat and tidy. After all, not everyone was organized like she was, and Maeve had so many other amazing qualities going for her. Besides, she seemed to have learned her lesson after her "lost in the Big Apple" adventure, and she was clearly making an effort to be more organized. She got up as soon as the alarm went off. She'd even settled on her outfit, a pair of wild striped pants and a solid white blouse, after only fifteen minutes. And remembering her aching feet from the day before, she gratefully slipped on the comfortable shoes Charlotte had insisted upon. It was small step for mankind, but a giant leap for Maeve.

"Come on, girls!" Mr. Taylor called. "The adventure is about to begin!" Katani and Maeve smiled. If he only knew, thought Katani.

Katani, Maeve, Mr. Taylor, and Sam ate a quick breakfast at a Manhattan deli. "It's part of the New York experience," Mr. Taylor said. Within half an hour, they were sitting comfortably on a ferry headed for Ellis Island. Mr. Taylor explained that Ellis Island was where thousands of immigrants from Europe arrived over a century before to seek a better life in America.

The wet wind on their faces and gentle rocking of the boat soothed them as they bumped over the harbor waves. "It's like flying!" Sam exclaimed gleefully, lifting his face into the spray. "Like being at the controls of a B-52—those were old World War II planes. Three, two, one, blast off!"

Maeve was so elated that she wasn't in the least bit bothered by Sam's WWII chatter. In fact, after everything that happened yesterday Maeve found it kind of cute. She wished her weekend would go on and on. She didn't even mind that Ellis Island was an educational place … she just hoped it wouldn't be *too* educational!

"Whoa—there's the Statue of Liberty!" Sam shouted a few minutes later. Sure enough, the ferry was headed toward Liberty Island, home of the Statue of Liberty, to drop off tourists there. Maeve and Katani stared in awe at the huge, beautiful statue of the lady with the torch who had welcomed so many to the shores of this country.

"Wow!" Katani said to Maeve. "She's so beautiful. I just never knew that she would be that beautiful."

Maeve nodded. "And much bigger than you'd expect."

"Did you know," Sam said, "that you can climb up to Lady Liberty's spiked cap? There are lots of stairs inside. I bet it's a mile high!"

"And I'll bet you have to be pretty fit to get there!" Mr.

Taylor laughed. "I tried it once—got halfway up and I was wiped! And that was a while ago … when I was still in shape!"

"Well, I'm gonna get in shape so I can run all the way!" Sam boasted.

Mr. Taylor laughed again. "Running, huh? Mighty ambitious of you, son."

Sam went on, "*Dad*, come on! I'm going to be an Army dude right? And if you are in the Marines or the Navy SEALS or the Army Rangers you HAVE to run all the way up. I think it's the law …"

"OK, Sam," Mr. Taylor said. "But you might want to do a little more research just to be on the safe side."

Maeve and Katani smiled at each other. Little brothers could be so weird, but very entertaining.

Twenty minutes later, the motor of the ferry slowed to a low hum. "Here we are!" Mr. Taylor announced. He helped the girls and Sam down onto the dock on Ellis Island. Signs everywhere directed them toward the main building, and they trailed in along with dozens of others.

Maeve groaned when she saw that the signs read: "Immigration Museum."

"Museum?" she whispered to Katani. "Is that code for 'boring', or what?"

"Maybe it won't be so bad," Katani whispered back. "I can't wait to hear about the Museum of Fine Arts adventure."

"But this isn't art, it's history!" Maeve insisted. "My worst subject, next to math."

She was already worried about the thrilled, absorbed look on Sam's face as he walked next to her. If Sam loved it, it was a sure bet that Maeve would hate it!

The tour started with a movie that talked about all the immigrants who came on ships, often with nothing but the clothes on their backs, dreaming of a new life here in America. The movie explained about the hardship of crossing the Atlantic and the difference between the wealthy passengers who could afford luxurious suites and the working class people who were crammed four to a cabin and often had to share their quarters with rats. A lot of the time, a family could afford passage for only one person, usually the father, who came to America, worked very hard to save money, and then sent for the rest of his family to join him. This could take years.

Then the movie went on to talk about Ellis Island itself—how it was the port through which the immigrants were processed, how their long European names were often misunderstood and misspelled by Customs officials who stamped their papers, and how consequently, they ended up with new, Anglicized names that were easier to spell but that had never belonged to them before.

Of course, the immigrants had to get jobs as soon as possible, but many were discriminated against in this new home where they hoped their lives would be better. The film showed signs in shop windows: "No Irish Need Apply."

Maeve looked at the jiggling, black-and-white footage of the people going through the immigration lines and felt a connection to these people. What did they have except hope? And yet, with nothing but that, they sailed across a dangerous ocean and started from scratch in a country where most of them couldn't even speak the language, and often the best jobs they could get were in sweatshops where they sewed or did laundry or other menial work for ten to twelve hours a day. They had no unions to protect their working conditions, and the bosses paid their men practically nothing—the children and women even less. Still, they came to America in droves and felt they were making things better for their families.

And they did, Maeve told herself. She knew that somewhere back in her family was a relative who came to America from Ireland. Suddenly she understood why. And just as suddenly, she had no more worries that this would be a boring day.

When the movie was over, the guide called out, "Come see our Immigrant Wall of Honor! You may even see the name of someone you know."

"Let's take a look, girls," Mr. Taylor invited them. "You know, Katani, Maeve's great-grandmother—my grandmother—came here from Ireland during the Great Depression in the 1930s. She had a pretty rough time. But I sure am glad she stuck it out!"

They followed the other tourists outside where the Wall of Honor was filled with names. Soon they could hear others oohing and aahing as they found familiar names.

"I've got it!" Sam shouted. "Right here, near the bottom!"

He pointed to a tiny line of carving. The others bent down to look. Sure enough, it said "John Taylor."

"Good, Sam," Mr. Taylor praised him. "And could you find your great-grandmother, Maeve Reilly?"

This time it was Katani who found the name further down the wall among the Rs. "There she is!" she exclaimed, pointing carefully at the name on the wall. Sam and Maeve put their fingers on it too. It made them feel more connected to the woman who had come all the way from Ireland so long ago.

"Our Maeve was named for her, of course," Mr. Taylor told Katani as they sat down in the food court for lunch. "In fact, Maeve, I have something for you. I thought this would be a good place to give it to you."

He reached into the inside pocket of his coat and brought out a soiled envelope. He looked at it for a moment, then passed it across to Maeve. "Here, honey."

Maeve took the envelope curiously. She had no idea what it was, or why her father wanted her to have it. The postmark on the envelope was written in faded blue ink, and though it was almost illegible, Maeve did see that it was addressed to "Mrs. Reilly" in County Cork, Ireland.

She looked at the return address. In even fainter letters, it said: "M. Reilly, New York, New York." Maeve felt quick tears sting her eyes. "It's from my great-grandmother," she said.

"Yes, it is," her father said. "It's a pretty special letter."

Maeve fumbled with the envelope and drew out a sheet of discolored paper that seemed very fragile with the passing of time. Carefully unfolding it, she glanced at the cramped handwriting inked across the page, hesitated, and then began: *"Dear Mother, It has been only a month since I arrived here in New York, but it seems so much longer without you. I did not realize a girl of seventeen still needs her mother so much, and having an ocean between us makes it so hard."*

Maeve shook her head a little, trying to clear out all the emotion. Everyone at the table was motionless, even Sam. Their eyes were intent on her. She took a deep breath and continued reading. *"I have been fortunate to obtain work right away in the same office building as my friend Maud. I clean all the floors below ten, and Maud cleans all the floors ten and above."*

Katani shook her head in disbelief. "Wow! She was a cleaning woman. And only seventeen ..."

Maeve went on. *"Here in New York, my education does not impress anyone. I had to take whatever job I could, and I'm thankful I could get it. It pays five dollars a week, which pays for my room. It's not much of a room—a sixth floor walkup, cold water,* of course, and cockroaches, so many cockroaches—but it's a roof over my head, and I'm thankful for that, too."

Maeve glanced around the table. No one spoke; no one even breathed. They were all hanging on the words of the girl who wrote this letter so long ago. *"I did have a bit of luck, though, on the voyage over. I met a young man who also came from Ireland to make his fortune in New York. His name is John Taylor, and he's already asked me to marry him.*

Of course, John is not able to support a wife yet. He earns only seven dollars a week working on the construction site downtown, but it's steady work, so far. He's a good worker and willing to do whatever they ask, so they may keep him on for awhile. But work is hard to find and keep these days—there's a depression on, everyone always reminds me—and it may be years before John and I can get married. It will be much longer, I know, before we can afford a flat for ourselves. We may live in one room, but it will be under our own steam, and I'm fine with that.

The air in New York always smells sooty, nothing like the crisp, clean air of Cork. I miss that, and I miss you and my brothers, Mother. Please tell them not to worry—even though I'd like to marry John, I won't until I've earned enough to pay their passage over, as I promised before I left. I'll keep that promise.

I hope someday to see you again, Mother. Please write to me. And I'll write to you as often as I can afford the stamps. Your loving daughter, Maeve."

It was very quiet at the table when Maeve finished reading. Her eyes were swimming with tears. She felt as though she could hear the voice of her great-grandmother, that young, hopeful Irish girl. *How brave she was!* Maeve thought. *And how amazing, to come here and work with no expectations except to pay for her brothers to join her!*

Katani was moved also. "She was remarkable," she said at last. "Imagine! Living like that in a sixth floor walkup with cold water ..."

Mr. Taylor nodded. "Strangely enough, the very area she lived in later became a pretty fancy address right in Greenwich Village. If I'm not mistaken, Katani, it's only a few blocks from where your cousin Michelle lives now."

Katani began to smile. "I'll bet Maeve Reilly would have thought that was pretty funny."

Mr. Taylor smiled too. "She had a wonderful sense of humor, though it's not apparent in that letter. I heard stories about her youth when I was a boy. I always thought my nana was spunky and brave and wonderful. And Maeve is turning out to be just like her."

Katani looked at Maeve across the table. "She is, Mr. Taylor!" she declared with conviction. "She really is!"

THE PERFECT GIFTS

It was 2 o'clock when they took the ferry back from Ellis Island. Everyone was quieter than usual, thinking of the girl who had written that letter of hope so long ago. Maeve, who put the letter in her jacket pocket so she could feel it close to her, touched her pocket every so often, just to remind herself of the girl who had come before her.

Mr. Taylor suggested they do some shopping for souvenirs. Katani eagerly said yes; she was anxious to find something perfect for Kelley, as well as her other sisters and the rest of the BSG.

Together they browsed the vendors lining the streets, just as—Katani and Maeve imagined—the early immigrants had combed the streets, craving what the vendors offered yet unable to pay for it.

Sam, whose imagination was limited to famous military battles, had stopped thinking about Maeve Reilly. He was busy looking for a general's hat he could take home.

Mr. Taylor was looking for old movie posters he could frame as artwork and put in the lobby of his theater. Since the theater had been saved by the seventh-grade talent show, he was constantly thinking about new ways to educate his customers. Making them aware of great old movies, he thought, was the perfect way to educate.

Maeve and Katani looked through intriguing piles of hats, belts, sunglasses, hair ribbons, and funky watches for souvenirs. "This is perfect for Kelley!" Maeve declared, pulling out a coffee-table-sized book about the history of horses in New York.

"This too!" Katani said, holding up a miniature horse and carriage like those driven around Central Park.

"She'll love it!" Maeve laughed, picturing Kelley's face when Katani gave it to her.

Twenty minutes later, the girls had chosen a pair of gorgeous combs, decorated with sequins and emeralds, for Isabel's hair; a lined journal with a silhouette of the New York skyline and "NY State of Mind" written on it for Charlotte; and a New York Mets baseball cap for Avery. "We could never get a Yankees cap—they're the Red Sox's biggest rivals," Katani pointed out.

A short stop at Michelle's apartment, and then they were packed and ready to go. Katani and Maeve thanked Michelle profusely and told her they'd had the time of their lives.

Michelle laughed. "Well, listen, you're both welcome back any time—but only on one condition ... when you two are either debuting your first fashion line or going to your Broadway premiere, I expect to be mentioned in the 'Thank you' speech!"

"It's a deal!" Katani promised.

Everyone agreed they could make the quickest run back to Boston if Mr. Taylor would agree to take the main highway. "After Thursday, Dad," Maeve said sternly, "you should forget about retro roads and drive on the Interstate like everyone else."

"Hey," Sam chimed in, "how come we drive on parkways but park on driveways?"

The girls groaned. "Are you going to be like this all the way back to Brookline?" Maeve asked him.

"Maybe," Sam grinned, "But I think we should take the the Interstate too."

Maeve's mouth fell open.

"Yeah," he joked, "I don't think I could stand it if we had another flat and needed another *girl* to rescue us!"

"Hey!" Maeve cried. "Sally was amazing!"

"Humph," Sam sniffed. "I'd feel a lot better if I'd been saved by a real mechanic."

"Puhlease!" Maeve huffed. "Sally *is* a 'real' mechanic!"

Mr. Taylor grinned at his daughter. "He's eight, Maeve. Give him time. Eventually he'll find out that girls are pretty good to have around." Mr. Taylor turned toward the Interstate, and headed for home.

CHAPTER 20

ᘒ

A HERO'S WELCOME

"THAT WAS AN ABSOLUTELY AMAZING ADVENTURE," Charlotte declared Sunday night.

"Totally cool," Avery pronounced.

"Awesomely fabulous," Isabel added.

The BSG, finally together again, were sitting in the Tower exchanging stories of their weekend and sighing over Maeve and Katani's "excellent adventure," as Maeve had nicknamed it. Isabel was wearing the hair combs they'd brought her, Charlotte clasped the journal in her arms, and Avery already sported the Mets cap over her straight black hair.

Maeve and Katani regaled their friends with the misadventures and highlights of their trip to New York. At one point Avery laughed so hard at Maeve for not recognizing Simon Blackstone that Maeve threw Happy Lucky Thingy at her. Marty went completely insane and tried to wrestle Happy Lucky away from Avery. That, of course, sent all the BSG into a frenzy of giggles that did not stop until Avery let go of Happy Lucky. After Maeve described in detail Simon kissing her hand, as well as his spur-of-the-moment concert, Charlotte

✿

decided that they needed to make a BSG reality show to save their stories and adventures for when they were older.

"My dad says my mother used to call things 'swoony' if they were just to die for," Charlotte volunteered, "and what happened to you, Maeve, is 100 percent swoony. Imagine having your hand kissed by Simon Blackstone—wow! You HAVE to tell this story on video. You can show it to your kids when you are older."

"Much better than being hugged by Danny Pellegrino," Avery said, and Isabel choked.

"Thanks a lot," she sputtered when she could talk. "It's not exactly like I planned that."

"Nope—you just were more afraid of the mummies than you were of Danny!" Avery laughed. Isabel threw a sequined pillow at her.

Avery ducked and then said to Maeve, "Admit it, Maeve. You'll never wash that hand again, right?"

Maeve grinned. "Well, I'm tempted, but if I don't, I'll have to wear a glove ... permanently!"

"Good point," Isabel shuddered.

"Yeah, we get the picture," Charlotte said.

"Anyway, if Rini actually does come to Boston like she says, I could end up in her music video—and who'd cast a girl with one gloved hand?" Maeve asked practically.

The girls laughed. Katani fished around in her bag and brought out something wrapped in brown paper, which she handed to Avery. "For you, Ave."

Avery opened the brown paper and squealed out loud. "Oh, Katani! You got me Leah Kim's autograph!"

"And on a program from the show," Katani pointed out. "She wasn't showing her own collection, but I saw her backstage. When I told her you were a big fan, she was glad to sign it."

"Kgirl, I can't believe you!" Maeve exclaimed. "You kept the Leah Kim sighting a secret from me, too."

Katani grinned. "I figured it'd be a good surprise."

Avery clasped the program to her. "I'm going to frame it! This is so cool!"

"I think it's even cooler that Katani's scarf was such a big hit at the show," Isabel said.

"Well, I think that Katani ought to make more of them and sell them at Ms. Razzberry Pink's store," Charlotte suggested. "If they made such a splash at the show, can you imagine what they'd do here?"

"The problem is that if I sold them at Think Pink, they'd all have to be pink." Katani laughed, and then a mysterious look came over her face.

"Here we go—Kgirl's brain is churning," chuckled Isabel.

And it was. Katani suddenly had visions of pink scarves in different hues and textures hanging from the windows at Think Pink.

"It's been a 'happily ever after' weekend," Maeve said dreamily. "Everything just fell into place, even though there were some rough spots along the way."

"I know what you mean," Katani said. "If anyone ever tries to get me to model again, drag me away, pronto!"

"At least Danny's backed off some," Charlotte said. "It was a pretty, should I say 'sticky' trip to the museum, but it's worth it if he gives Izzy some space … finally."

"Who knows?" Isabel wondered. "Poor Danny, he didn't realize that he just had to give us some space and then we'd miss him."

The other girls gave good imitations of being sick. Isabel laughed. "I was kidding! But it does feel good not to worry

❀

anymore that he's going to be popping up everywhere I go."

"I still say," Charlotte murmured, "that he and Betsy are a match made in heaven."

But nobody else was listening. They were looking at the lovely gifts Maeve and Katani had brought back and marveling over one of the best weekends ever …

ℭℛ

Charlotte's Journal:

I just had to start this new journal tonight! Maeve and Katani gave it to me—it's got a great New York logo on it and a picture of the skyline—and I'm going to keep it for my secret thoughts and special dreams … like this one: wouldn't it be wonderful if the BSG could go on an incredibly great adventure with my dad and me?

The truth is that as much as I loved hearing about their weekend, Maeve's letter from her grandmother was what really touched my heart. It was so sweet that we all almost cried. I'm definitely going online tomorrow to see what I can find out about Ellis Island, and the next time I'm in New York I am NOT going to miss it! It sounds like something really special. Maybe I could do an article on it for The Sentinel.

Maeve's Notes to Self:

 Re-read Maeve Reilly's letter
tomorrow and any day I feel sorry for
myself. She didn't feel sorry for
herself, and her life was a lot harder
than mine! Yeah, I have the learning
disability thing, and I may always
have it. But you know what? I have
parents who care that I do well,
tutors to help me, and great friends
who remind me all the time that I
mean a lot to them. So lighten up, M
K-T—remember your great-grandmother
and think about how you can make her
proud.

Kgirl List:

Plan to Market Original Scarves

1. *Make at least a dozen more scarves in pink and different lengths. Talk to Ms. Razzberry Pink about selling them in the shop.*

2. *Talk to Candice about possibly selling them at a college market day at her school. Or how about making/selling them for different sororities, as a group thing? Maybe design a scarf all the girls of the same sorority could wear?*

3. *Design website for scarves and other original designs—call it KgirlFashions.com—a great way to start my empire!*

4. *Maybe Mr. Taylor would take 1 or 2 scarves to use as giveaways for contests at his theater?? Great publicity!*

Avery's Blog:

OK—big learning week.
 # 1 lesson for me—never close the door behind you unless you check that you can unlock it first!

#1 for Katani—Being the center of attention and walking down a runway was not her thing. I could have told her that—she's happy as a clam when she's backstage taking charge! Kelley doesn't call her Miss Bossy for nothing!

So it was a great weekend. I scored an autograph from Leah Kim, my absolute favorite designer, and a Mets cap, which is great, because you can wear a Mets cap without practically getting in a fistfight with anyone at Fenway Park (except for Red Sox fans who remember Bill Buckner). Not the same with a Yankees cap!

P.S. I honestly wouldn't have missed my time with Char and Izzy at the museum, not even for that trip to New York, not even to meet Leah Kim. I have a feeling that without me along, they'd have gone bonkers *in there …*

☙

To be continued …

New BSG special adventure!

charlotte in paris

Charlotte returns to Paris to search for her long lost cat and to visit her best Parisian friend, Sophie. When a stolen Picasso sketch ends up in Charlotte's backpack, the BSG's bon voyage gifts become the detective tools for solving the mystery.

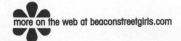

more on the web at beaconstreetgirls.com

fashion frenzy Book Extras

Book Club Buzz

10 QUESTIONS FOR YOU AND YOUR FRIENDS TO CHAT ABOUT

1. What is the best way for a girl in Isabel's position to let someone know that she needs her space?

2. Do you have an idol or hero? Who and why?

3. How is New York City a special place for each of the Beacon Street Girls? What is the most exciting part about New York City to you?

4. Do you think that Katani's decision about which Beacon Street Girl to bring on her trip was fair? Why or why not?

5. Why does Katani become frustrated during the trip down the Merritt Parkway?

6. How are field trips different from learning in the classroom? What was your favorite field trip and why?

7. What do the girls learn from Sally the mechanic?

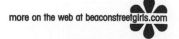

8. How do Maeve and Katani demonstrate their different talents and individual strengths at the fashion show?
9. What would you like to talk about on a TV interview exclusive?
10. How did your ancestors come to America? Did they set foot on Ellis Island, like Maeve's great-grandparents?

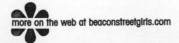

Nests are so happy comfy!

Charlotte Ramsey

Charlotte's Word Nerd Dictionary

BSG Words

Cling-on: (p. 98) noun—an unwanted person who follows someone around
Swoony: (p. 198) adjective—dreamiest and most romantic

Spanish Words and Phrases ...

Que?: (p.11)—What?
¿Cómo estás?: (p. 97)—How are you?
¿Adónde va usted?: (p.99)—Where are you going?

Other Cool Words ...

De jour: (p. 2) adjective—a French expression meaning 'of the day'; ex: soup de jour
Lament: (p. 28) verb—to express sorrow or regret
Luminous: (p. 44) adjective—full of light
Listlessly: (p. 46) adverb—lethargically, lacking energy
Boisterous: (p. 60) adjective—loud, noisy, and lacking in discipline

Garish: (p. 61) adjective—loud and flashy, gaudy

Extol: (p. 64) verb—to praise highly

Aloft: (p. 77) adjective—high or higher up

Sarcophagus: (p. 91) noun—a stone coffin, often inscribed or decorated with sculpture

Hieroglyphics: (p. 94) noun—the system of writing, such as that of ancient Egypt, which uses pictorial symbols

Artillery: (p. 97) noun—supply of instruments used for purposes of attack or defense

Muster: (p. 104) verb—to summon up

Mod: (p. 125) noun—an unconventionally modern style of fashionable dress originating in England in the 1960s.

Lavish: (p. 126) adjective—splendid and extravagant

Amend: (p. 133) verb—to correct

Ambitious: (p. 142) adjective—having a strong desire for success or achievement

Flabbergasted: (p. 142) adjective—as if struck dumb with astonishment and surprise

Haphazard: (p. 164) adjective—marked by great carelessness

Menial: (p. 190) adjective—relating to work or a job regarded as undignified

Drove: (p.191) noun—a large mass of people moving as a body

Definitions adapted from *Webster's Dictionary*, Fourth Edition, Random House.

 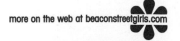

fashion frenzy **trivialicious trivia**

1. What interests Anna the most about the Ancient Egyptians?
    A. Fashion
    B. Music
    C. Makeup
    D. Mummies

2. Who changes the flat tire of Mr. Taylor's car?
    A. Sam
    B. The state trooper
    C. Mr. Taylor
    D. Sally

3. Where does Katani go to get directions to Michelle's apartment?
    A. The *Teen Beat* Magazine offices
    B. New York City tourist information booth
    C. A gas station off the Merritt Parkway
    D. A Korean deli in Greenwich Village

4. What did Betsy Fitzgerald write about when she won an essay contest in third grade?
    A. Egyptian pyramids
    B. Egyptian cosmetics
    C. Egyptian music
    D. Egyptian gods

5. Where does Maeve get lost when she is all alone in New York City?
    A. Times Square
    B. Central Park
    C. Greenwich Village
    D. The Empire State Building

6. What is the name of the action movie starring the man who rescues Maeve?

A. *Hip-hop Hero*
B. *The Swashbuckler*
C. *Rock Nation*
D. *Diminitron*

7. What happens to the model that Katani replaces?

A. She chickens out
B. She is fired for saying mean things about Maeve
C. She gets food-poisoning
D. She oversleeps

8. Who made the piece of jewelry that Katani uses to save the day for Dina B?

A. Katani
B. Kelley
C. Isabel
D. Ms. Razzberry Pink

9. What was Maeve's great-grandmother's job when she first came to America?

A. Cleaning woman
B. Nanny
C. Dressmaker
D. Baker

10. What did Mr. Taylor buy as a New York souvenir?

A. Army garb for Sam
B. A bracelet for Maeve's mom
C. A postcard from Ellis Island
D. Movie posters for his theater

be happy  be lucky